DATE DUE

CARTWHEEL

A Sequel to Double Eagle

by

SNEED B. COLLARD III

Distributed by Mountain Press Publishing Company, Missoula, Montana
1-800-234-5308
www.mountain-press.com

Cover and Book Design by Kathleen Herlihy-Paoli, Inkstone.
The text of this book is set in ITC Berkeley.
Printed on 30% post-consumer waste recycled paper.

Collard, Sneed B.
Cartwheel : a sequel to Double Eagle / Sneed B. Collard III. -- 1st ed.
    p. cm.
SUMMARY: Friends Mike Gilbert and Kyle Daniels reunite for a cross-country thriller involving drag racing, the rescue of Kyle's sister Annie, and a quest to find a priceless 1964 silver dollar.
    LCCN 2012910635
    ISBN 978-0-9844460-3-2

    [1. Coins--Collectors and collecting--Fiction. 2. Adventure and adventurers--Fiction. 3. Coming of age--Fiction. 4. Automobiles, Racing--Fiction. 5. Runaways--Fiction. 6. Detective and mystery stories.]
    I. Collard, Sneed B. Double eagle. II. Title.

    PZ7.C67749Car 2013   [Fic]
    QBI12-600134

Manufactured in the United States of America
10 9 8 7 6 5 4 3 2 1

Images of 1964 Peace dollar courtesy and copyright © Daniel Carr.
Cover image of 1957 Bel Air © iStock Images.
Page 8 image: Photo of Bliss Press at the Denver Mint courtesy of Michael P. Lantz.

Bucking Horse Books
MISSOULA, MONTANA

For my brother Eric Dawson, who's always got my back.

—Sneed

THE UNITED STATES MINT

Denver, Colorado
May 17th, 1965

The pressman stood in front of the enormous World War II era machine. The towering gray press once spit out millions of deadly bullets. Now, it made money. As the machine rumbled and whirred and clanked, the pressman placed lightly-oiled, one-ounce silver blanks— or planchets—into coin feeder tubes, a handful at a time. The man watched as the machine's feed fingers picked up two of the planchets and automatically placed them into separate steel collars on the machine.

THUNK.

With 120 tons of pressure, the machine's massive ram slammed onto the two silver blanks, instantly transforming them into a pair of brand new, gleaming silver dollars, or "cartwheels". As the mechanism rose back up, the feed fingers ejected the new coins into a small catch box in the back of the machine. Then, they loaded two more blanks into the steel collars.

Even though the pressman wore foam earplugs, the noise in the room was almost deafening. It was not loud enough, however, to drown out the hammering of the man's heart as he glanced at the other Mint employees around him. Everyone was busy. Only a few feet away, another man fed silver blanks into a second giant silver-dollar-making machine. Other workers drove small vehicles to haul away the finished cartwheels in green tote boxes and bring new planchets in for production. The press room foreman paced back and forth, studying each moving part to make sure it functioned properly, while off to the side a pair of Mint Police watched to confirm that every operation followed the strict security rules of the United States Department of the Treasury.

This isn't going to be easy, the pressman thought to himself, *but time is on my side.* And suddenly, his opportunity arrived.

With a loud crack, one of the coin dies on the machine next to him exploded. The dies held the designs that were stamped into the coin blanks, but they regularly needed to be replaced. This one shattered into a dozen pieces.

"Shut it down!" the foreman hollered.

Everyone hurried over to the second machine. And with all eyes focused away from him, the pressman seized his chance. He quickly circled around to the back of his machine and dipped his hand into the coin catch box. He slid a single silver dollar inside his sleeve while dropping an old, worn silver dollar into the larger green tote box below. Then, as he joined his co-workers at the other coin press, he transferred the new silver dollar to his pocket.

A die setter quickly replaced the damaged coin die on the second machine, and within minutes, everyone resumed work. Three hours later, the pressman's shift ended. Along with his co-workers, he walked to the front of the Mint building, where a security guard checked his lunch box and bid him good-night.

"See you tomorrow," he told several other Mint employees as he trotted down the steps onto Colfax Avenue and headed to the nearest corner to cross the street.

As he walked, the noise of the coin presses still rang in the pressman's ears, but his lips curled into a smile.

I did it, he thought to himself. *I pulled it off. That coin dealer is going to be mighty happy. So will my wife—with the cash.*

Between his excitement and the ringing in his ears, he didn't notice the bus. The bus driver was running four minutes behind schedule and hoping to make it up by the end of his route. As the pressman stepped off the curb, the fourteen-ton vehicle didn't even have time to brake. It slammed into the man at full speed, killing him instantly.

He died with a smile on his face.

Pensacola, Florida
June, 1975

ONE

I don't know why the growl of the car doesn't register in my brain. Zeus—the god of sky and thunder—probably has something to do with it. Every afternoon since I arrived in Florida two weeks ago, violent storms have pummeled the Pensacola region, hurling countless lightning bolts from the sky, rattling our windows with blast after blast of cannon-fire thunder. It's possible that the current bombardment drowns out the sounds of the powerful engine outside.

But a more likely reason I don't hear the car drive up is the article on page four of my hot-off-the-presses *Coin Universe* newspaper.

The article, titled "The Last of the Peace Dollars", talks about something I've never heard anything about—how, in 1965, the United States Treasury secretly minted hundreds of thousands of silver dollars. Real ones. Just like in the old days.

And this is big news to me.

Like many coin collectors, I have a special fascination with silver dollars. For a sixteen year-old without a steady job, the large silver "cartwheels" are worth a lot of money—up to five bucks for an ordinary specimen. But there's more to it than that. When I gaze down at old-time Morgan or Peace dollars in a coin shop display case, visions of Wild West gunfights, gambling, and steam-powered locomotives fill my head. It's like history is reaching out and, as my dad would say, grabbing me by the chest hairs.

Part of the attraction is that the United States Mint

stopped making silver dollars way back in 1935, during the Great Depression. Or so I thought. Now, halfway through the article, I discover that during the early 1960s, senators from the great state of Montana twisted every arm in Washington, D.C. to get the Treasury to mint brand-new silver dollars.

I am just about to learn the rest of the story when the doorbell jolts my concentration. At that exact same moment, my new baby brother, who has napped peacefully through the entire thunderstorm, wakes up with a blood-curdling shriek.

"Mike, can you get the door?" my stepmother Paula's tired voice calls from the other room.

"Uuuuuh," I groan, closing the *Coin Universe* and rolling off the bed.

I walk down the hallway, passing the nursery where I glimpse my stepmother rocking my half-brother, trying to get him to calm down. The sight does not fill me with warm fuzzy feelings. Every time I see them together, I smolder over yet another drastic Life Change that has been forced on me without my permission. But as usual, I stuff those feelings as I walk through our dimly-lit living room and open the front door.

Down off the porch I see a guy with his back to me. He is gazing up at the storm clouds or, perhaps, the canopy of oak trees that spreads over our yard. Beyond the man, parked on our semi-circular red-dirt driveway, sits an old beat-up two-door sedan. I'm no car guy, but I think it might be some kind of Chevrolet, and it has definitely seen better days.

"Yes?" I say in a voice not altogether friendly. The feelings about my stepmother and brother have darkened my mood, and I am eager to escape back into the silver dollar article without wasting time chatting with a stranger.

When the guy turns around, I instinctively tense up. The man isn't that tall—about my own height of five-eight, five-nine—but underneath his T-shirt, I make out rippling shoulder, arm, and chest muscles. If I had to guess, I'd say the guy has twenty-five, thirty pounds on me. I've started taking some martial arts, but can't help thinking that in a fight this stranger could swat away my kung-fu moves like a gorilla swatting away a mosquito.

His pale blue eyes, however, disturb me even more than his muscles. Like lasers, they cut through the dim light of the overcast afternoon. Then, I realize that there's something familiar about those eyes.

It isn't until his mouth spreads into a cocky smile that I finally recognize him.

"Kyle!"

TWO

"What are you doing here?" I step off the porch, hardly noticing the rainwater soaking into my bare feet. Kyle takes my hand in a firm grip.

"How ya doin', Mike?"

A grin plastered across my face, I study him. Kyle's blonde hair is darker now, and even longer than before, reaching almost to his shoulders. His posture, crankshaft straight, still carries the same confidence as always. But there is no doubt about it. At seventeen, Kyle has almost become a man. He wears a two-day growth of reddish-blonde stubble on his face, and his bright blue eyes have lost the last trace of, well, *dependence* they carried when we parted company during a Category 4 hurricane two years ago.

If I wasn't a year younger than Kyle and didn't know him so well, I would feel hopelessly inferior in his presence. Now, I am just happy to see him.

"I can't believe you're here."

He chuckles and scratches the whiskers on his cheek. "Me, neither. I was on my way up to Birmingham and thought I'd stop, see if I could find you."

"I tried to write you after the hurricane," I tell him.

"The letters probably got returned, huh?"

I nod, then step to the side. "You want to come in?"

On cue, the unhappy wailing of my baby brother gusts through the open front door.

Kyle motions toward the house. "What's that? Bob-cats?"

I laugh. "I wish. My dad got married since I last saw you. That's my new brother."

Kyle processes this information, then cocks his head toward his car. "Hey. How 'bout we go for a ride?"

He doesn't need to ask twice.

I bound into the house and poke my head into the nursery. My brother is starting to quiet down as my stepmother, face sagging with sleep deprivation, nurses him. I avert my eyes from this embarrassing situation.

"I'm going out with a friend," I tell her.

Paula looks up, surprise in her voice. "What friend? Really?"

I don't blame her for the question. Even though this is my fifth summer in Florida, I haven't exactly bonded with the locals. It's my fault as much as anyone else's. My time here passes so quickly, it hardly seems worth the effort to try to meet anyone. In fact, the only real friend I've ever made during the summers with my dad happens to be standing right outside.

"His name's Kyle Daniels," I explain. "My dad knows him."

"Does—" Paula starts to ask another question, but decides not to, either because she's too exhausted or concludes that it isn't any of her business—which it isn't.

"I'll be back in a couple of hours," I tell her.

"Okay. Have fun."

I grab a ten-dollar bill from my room and shove it into my front shorts pocket. Sandals on, I hurry out the door.

Kyle is already behind the old Chevy's steering wheel, smoking a cigarette. He reaches across and flings the opposite door open for me. As I slide into the front passenger seat, he twists the key in the ignition.

"Holy Crap!" I shout as the engine roars like a pissed-off lion. "What is this thing, anyway?"

Kyle flashes me a satisfied grin. "A '57 Bel Air, with a few extra odds and ends. A big block engine instead of the original small block. A Muncie 4-speed M-22 'Rock Crusher' transmission. New heads, cam-shaft, and valve springs. Beefier suspension. Couple 'a other things."

Kyle is speaking a foreign language to me, but as his left foot pushes in the clutch, I do notice him shoving a strange-looking stick forward. It's shaped like a "T" and he hardly has to move it to change gears.

"What's with the stick shift?"

"It's called a Hurst shifter, for racing," he explains. "It makes the distance between gears a lot shorter, so you can shift faster. We get onto a bigger road, I'll show you."

We rumble out of our driveway and onto our red clay street. Within a couple of blocks, Kyle finds blacktop and gives the Bel Air a little juice. I feel my body press back into the seat as the vehicle surges forward.

"Where did you get this car?" I ask, impressed.

"Built it." As he stubs out his cigarette in the ashtray, I notice grease stains on his fingers and scarred knuckles. "I've been workin' in a garage down in Tampa, but the guy who owns it lets me work on my own stuff in my free time."

"And you race it? Drag racing?"

Kyle brakes at a STOP sign. "Which way?"

"Go right," I tell him.

He spins the wheel and accelerates. "I keep the body rusty and ragged. The other guys see it and think they're goin' to clean my clock. When we get to the startin' line, I gotta surprise waitin' for 'em."

To demonstrate, Kyle punches the gas and I feel like I am blasting off from Cape Canaveral. Within seconds we top fifty miles per hour and the wind whips my face like a starting flag.

Kyle points to a tachometer on the dash. It reads 5000 RPMs—the engine speed. "We're not even out of second gear!" Kyle shouts over the roar of the pistons. Then, he eases off the pedal and we coast to the stoplight ahead.

I direct him down Ninth Avenue, to the towering orange-and-white A-frame of a Whataburger restaurant. People stare as we pull the Bel Air into the parking lot, but Kyle is evidently used to it. Inside, I buy us lunch at the counter and we carry it to a corner table.

"So," I ask him, extracting three slimy, disgusting pickles from my burger. "You're on your way to Birmingham? What for?"

Kyle's mouth already bulges with a slurry of cheeseburger and fries. "Goin' to see my sister."

"Annie? She's in Birmingham?"

"Mike, me and you got a lot to catch up on."

I shove some fries into my mouth and wait for him to continue.

"Mama died 'bout a year ago," he tells me.

"Aw, man." I have never received news like this from anyone—especially anyone my age—and am not sure how to respond.

"Yeah." He nods, taking another bite, his face carefully masking any emotions.

"What about Ray?"

"Gone."

"Geez. I'm sorry."

Kyle shrugs. "Anyway, I dropped out of school and got a full-time job at the garage, told the courts I'd take care of Annie."

"They wouldn't let you?"

Kyle shakes his head. "Said I wasn't old enough."

"Wait," I say. "They let you keep living on your own, but wouldn't let you watch Annie?"

"That's right. They sent her to live with my aunt and uncle up in Birmingham."

"This is the same aunt and uncle you visited in Mobile a couple of summers ago?"

"That's them. They moved up to Birmingham right after the hurricane."

As he talks and chews, Kyle's eyes are focused, but they aren't looking anywhere particular. I can tell he is thinking hard about what's happened.

"But isn't that better?" I venture. "You and Annie both liked your aunt, didn't you?"

He again shrugs and takes another bite, washing it down with some chocolate shake. "My aunt was alright. It's just that..."

"What?"

"Nothin', Mike. I just feel I ought to go see her, that's all."

Before I can ask him anything more, he says, "So what about you? You got a new stepmother and brother? How's that goin'?"

The truth is that it stinks—literally, a lot of the time. Kyle's story puts my own troubles in perspective, however. "Well," I tell him, popping a fry in my mouth. "It's not my first choice."

"What's your stepmom's name? She nice?"

"Paula. She tries, but my brother David takes all her time. And my dad…well, it's not the same as it was."

"Never is," Kyle says matter-of-factly.

"You're lucky you caught me at home. Usually, I go out to the lab."

"What you do out there?"

"Different things. My dad's been collecting all these samples of sargassum weed out in the Gulf of Mexico."

"Sargassum weed," Kyle muses. "Ain't that the stuff the hippies smoke?"

"Uh, no. It's—" I begin to tell him, but then catch the twinkle in his eyes. I laugh. "Good one. No. Sargassum is this kind of algae that floats around out in the Gulf and has all of these animals living with it. My dad's paying me to sort through the samples and count up the contaminants he finds in them."

"Like pollution?"

"Yeah. There's this factory somewhere in Louisiana that keeps dumping millions of little floating plastic pellets that end up out in the ocean. My dad's worried baby sea turtles and other animals might be eating them."

"That ain't good."

I shake my head and slosh down some chocolate shake. "Nope. Anyway, when I'm not doing that, I usually go over to the library and read, or see if any new stamps have come out at the University post office."

Kyle's eyebrows lift. "What, you collectin' stamps now, too?"

"A little. I like coins better."

"I still got those coin albums you gave me before."

"Have you filled them up yet?"

He laughs. "No, but I sift through my change and

find a new date every once in a while."

We each take a bite of our burgers. Then, Kyle sits back and looks directly at me. I know what he's going to ask next.

"So, Mike. You still got it?"

I nod. "It's back at my mom's house in Santa Barbara, locked up in an old Wells Fargo strongbox my uncle gave me."

"You ever told anyone about it?"

"Not a soul. What about you? You got yours?" As I ask the question, I realize I am half holding my breath.

Kyle also nods. "I got it hidden away in Tampa. I ain't never told nobody about it neither."

I exhale. "Good. I was afraid you might have sold it."

Kyle grins. "I can listen. You told me to hang onto it. I hung onto it."

The 'its' we are talking about are two little items that only Kyle and I know about. And I have thought about them every day for the last two years.

THREE

When we first met, Kyle and I were spending the summer on Shipwreck Island in southern Alabama. My dad was teaching summer school at the brand new marine lab on the eastern tip of the island, and Kyle's stepfather Ray headed the lab's maintenance department. After a rocky start, Kyle and I became fast friends. We played pool together. We went fishing together. We learned to trust each other.

We also made a discovery.

In an old Civil War fort next to the lab, we tracked down a previously unknown cache of twenty-dollar gold coins, or double eagles, minted by the Confederate States of America. Unfortunately, we happened to make our discovery just as the worst hurricane in fifty years slammed into southern Alabama. Even more unfortunate, we weren't alone. One of the other professor's wives and her lover—a student of my dad's—ambushed us in the fort and tried to steal the gold.

Kyle and I managed to escape with our lives—and one double eagle each. The professor's wife and her lover…they weren't so lucky.

As eighty mile-per-hour gusts of wind battered our faces, Kyle and I said goodbye to each other. Then, we fled the island with our respective families. It was a good thing too, because Hurricane Elsa flattened the fort, much of the marine lab, and the bridge leading to the mainland.

After the hurricane, I tried to find Kyle, but his family moved with no forwarding address. I didn't hear from him again until he showed up on my doorstep an hour ago.

Now, sitting in the Whataburger restaurant, Kyle asks me, "So what are we going to do with these things?"

I glance around and lower my voice. "The double eagles? Are you desperate for money?"

He shakes his head. "I'm doin' okay."

"Then I think we should keep hanging onto them. These are the only Confederate gold pieces anyone has *ever* found, and the rest of the world still doesn't know they exist. The longer we hold them, the more valuable they're going to become."

Kyle nods appreciatively. "How much you think they're worth now?"

I whistle. "I don't know, but I think about it every day."

"Guess."

I wash down the last of my fries with a slug of milk-shake. "I don't know...half a million each?"

Kyle coughs. "Serious?"

"It could be more. A lot more."

We sit silently for a few moments. Then I ask him something I've wanted to ask ever since the hurricane. "Kyle, after the hurricane, the police came to see me. They asked about Rod and Becky."

"What'd you tell 'em?"

"I stuck to our story. I told them Rod and Becky were lovers and they were following us when the fort caved in."

"That's pretty much the truth, ain't it?" Kyle asks.

"Yeah, except I said that we never found any gold."

"Which is *almost* the truth. Most of it got swept out into Mobile Bay by the storm, right?. So..."

I crush up my burger wrapper and shove it into the

French fries container. "Well," I tell him. "I was just wondering if...if you ever feel bad about what happened to Rod and Becky?"

Kyle doesn't hesitate. "*Hell* no. Mike, they pulled a gun on us! Far as I'm concerned, when that fort collapsed, they got what they deserved. Why? You feelin' guilty about them?"

I meet Kyle's eyes. "That's the funny thing. I don't. But I keep thinking I should."

Kyle and I stare at each other for a moment. Then, at the same time, we grin. Suddenly, the past two years vanish.

Almost like they never happened.

By the time we return to my house, my dad's green International pickup truck sits cooling in the driveway. As we're getting out of Kyle's car, my dad shuffles out to greet us wearing his official biologist uniform—faded Levi's, sandals, and a plain white T-shirt smelling of formaldehyde and 100% ethanol.

"Kyle Daniels!" he shouts enthusiastically.

Kyle grins and shakes his hand. "Hello, Professor."

"Come on in!" My dad steers Kyle toward our house, and inside, I smell food cooking.

"Can you stay for dinner?" my father asks.

Kyle and I look at each other, but neither of us admits to our late Whataburger lunch. "Sure," Kyle says. "That'd be fine."

Paula emerges from the kitchen and my father introduces her.

Then, my dad points to a squirming creature on the floor. "And this," he tells Kyle, "is Mike's little brother David."

David—or Booger Nose as I affectionately call him—is perched in a "baby tray" on the floor nearby. When he sees Kyle, he stops wriggling and stares intently at the new face. Kyle squats down next to him.

"Hey, man," Kyle says, extending a finger so that David can curl his hand around it. I can tell that, unlike me, Kyle actually likes babies. That surprises me until I remember how good he was with his sister Annie back on Shipwreck Island.

"What is he, about two months?" Kyle asks Paula.

"April 8th," Paula confirms.

"He's a big little guy."

Paula rolls her eyes. "Tell me about it. That kid never stops eating."

"That's good," Kyle tells David directly. "You eat as much as you can hold. Your brother and I will get you some barbeque tomorrow."

My dad and Paula laugh, but I'm pretty sure Kyle means it.

Before dinner, I show Kyle around the house and take him into the backyard where we keep our dogs, Stump and Shad, and our pens full of turtles.

"How many turtles you got?" he asks.

"About fifty," I repeat. "Every time it rains, we go out and rescue them from the roadways." I climb into one of the pens and pick up a box turtle. "See? I painted orange numbers on their shells to tell them apart."

"They all box turtles?"

"Naw. There's a couple of GTs."

Kyle's eyes twinkle. "Gran Torinos? You got cars in there?"

"Gopher tortoises," I say, realizing no one else understands the terminology my dad and I use with each other. "They're probably hiding under some of the logs."

Kyle studies the pens admiringly. "Annie'd love this. What's in the ponds?" he asks, nodding toward the small plastic pools we've sunk into the ground.

"That's a slider," I say, pointing to a yellow-and-green-striped head poking up out of the water. "There's also a musk turtle, a chicken turtle, and a couple of alligator snappers in there somewhere."

Kyle's eyebrows rise. "You got snappers?"

"Well, maybe only one now. We had a big one in here, maybe ten or twelve pounds, but we haven't seen him lately. I think he probably climbed over the fence."

"They can do that?"

I shrug. "Be careful where you walk."

Later, around the dinner table, my dad interrogates Kyle on what he's been up to. Kyle and my father always hit it off back on Shipwreck Island, and Kyle doesn't seem self-conscious about telling him about his mom's death and Ray taking off.

"I'm sorry to hear about that," my dad tells him. "You know, I was basically out on the street, too, at your age."

"No, sir. I didn't know that."

My father nods. "Instead of finding a job, I joined the Air Force."

"I thought about doin' somethin' like that," Kyle says, "but then I wouldn't be able to keep an eye on Annie."

"You're going to see her now?" Paula asks, inserting a bottle of warm milk into David's gaping maw.

"Yes, ma'am."

"Can you stay here tonight?" I ask hopefully. "It's getting pretty late."

Paula has cooked one of my favorite meals, shrimp gumbo. Kyle takes a big spoonful and ponders my question.

"Yeah," he says. "If I'm not puttin' y'all out."

"Not at all," Paula answers. "We're glad to have you."

Kyle takes another bite of gumbo, and I see his forehead furrow in concentration. Then, he looks at me. "I been thinkin', Mike. You want to ride up to Birmingham with me?"

As soon as he asks the question, I know my answer.

I turn to my dad. "Can I?"

A look of disappointment flashes through my father's eyes, and I can guess why. I spend the entire school year with my mother and stepfather in California. My dad and I, well, we only get eight weeks a year together and every day has always counted. On the other hand, things are different now with Paula and David here. I'm sure he feels it, too. He masks his reservations and says, "Sure. That sounds like a good plan. When will you be back?"

"A day or two," Kyle answers.

"Don't you have to get back to work?" I ask.

Kyle shrugs. "My boss likes me. He won't mind."

My father looks at me, Paula, and Kyle and forces a positive note. "I guess it's settled then."

FOUR

Before we leave the next morning, my dad pulls me aside and hands me three twenty-dollar bills.

Surprise silences me. Then, I tell him, "I've got money."

"I know, but you never know what might come up. I want you to take Kyle out for a couple of meals, too."

"Okay."

I've packed an extra shirt, underwear, and toothbrush in a small bag my dad calls an AWOL bag. I also throw in the new copy of the *Coin Universe* newspaper, along with the novel I'm reading—*Mila 18*, by my current favorite author, Leon Uris. I toss the AWOL bag in the back of the Bel Air and take my position in the front passenger seat.

As we pull out of the driveway, my dad calls to us, "Have a good time."

I wave to Paula and David, who is staring at a squirrel twenty feet above his head. Then, I look at my dad. Despite his apparent jolliness, I notice the same moist eyes I see when he puts me on the airplane at the end of each summer. I mouth the word "Bye" and give him his own wave.

Out on the highway, Kyle tells me, "I'm surprised you decided to come along. I mean, you don't get much time with your dad."

"It's different now," I tell him. "They're probably glad to have some time to themselves."

I don't know if I really believe that, but it helps justify my decision to go to Birmingham.

Kyle doesn't reply. He just checks the rearview mirror, punches the accelerator, and begins to show me the world at ninety miles-per-hour.

For normal earth-bound drivers, Birmingham's about a four-hour drive from Pensacola. Kyle and I make it in just over three.

At first I worry about cops, but Kyle seems to have a sixth sense for where they might be hiding out along the two-lane roads we start out on. Once we cross into Alabama and pick up I-65, one state trooper does follow us for a few miles, but Kyle spots him early and keeps the speedometer safely below the 55 mile-per-hour line. As soon as our escort pulls off, we roar back to business, my grin widening in direct proportion to our velocity. I relax, forget my conflicted feelings about my dad, and enjoy my new supersonic lifestyle.

Sailing through the Alabama countryside, Kyle and I fill in more details of the past couple of years. After he left Shipwreck Island with his family, he tells me, they moved to three or four different cities around the South—which is why my letters never caught up with him.

"Ray didn't get any better?" I ask over the roar of the wind blasting through the open windows.

"Naw," Kyle answers. "And he started drinkin', too."

Back on Shipwreck Island, Kyle had explained that his stepfather Ray had been a Korean War veteran, and had a lot of trouble dealing with other people—especially authority figures. Jobs didn't last long and whenever he lost one, Ray would insist they move to a new city.

"By the time we got to Tampa," Kyle tells me now, "Mama was about wore out. She just kept gettin' thinner and thinner, lookin' worse and worse. I thought it was all that movin' around."

"It wasn't?"

Kyle shakes his head. "Cancer. After she died, Ray couldn't handle it, and went off the deep end. Disappeared. We never saw him again. I already had a job so the courts gave me "Emancipated Minor" status, and let me stay. I tried to talk 'em into lettin' Annie stay with me, too. She wanted to," he says looking at me, one hand lightly resting on the steering wheel. "But it wasn't no use. All I had was this cheapskate public defender on my side, and I don't even think he cared what happened to us."

"How old is Annie now? Twelve?"

"Thirteen."

"Do you miss her?"

Kyle fishes around in his shirt pocket for his pack of cigarettes. "Yeah. She's not happy in Birmingham. That's why I'm goin' up there. Make sure she knows she's still got family."

"But your aunt and uncle are family, too," I point out.

"It's not the same."

Kyle shifts gears—and subjects. "So, you got a brother now, too. What's up with that?"

I shake my head and hold my hand out the window like a little wing, riding the air rushing by. "Don't ask me. I think my dad met Paula just before last summer, but he didn't tell me about her right away—which was easy because we spent most of the summer on Shipwreck Island, helping rebuild the lab after the hurricane. At the end of the summer I went back to California like usual. A month later my dad calls and tells me he's married. A month after that, Paula's pregnant."

Kyle chuckles. "They musta' been in a hurry."

"I guess."

"Well, at least Paula seems nice. And your brother. You may not like him now, but I'll bet you're glad to have him later."

I shrug.

"How're things in California?" Kyle asks next. "About the same? I forget, your stepdad's an attorney?"

"Accountant."

"You said before that he was an okay guy."

"I did? I'd have to revise that opinion. I really don't know why my mom married him."

"What's wrong with him?"

It was a good question, but difficult to answer.

"You know, when I first met him, I thought he was fine. Not too interesting, but not too bad either. Now..."

"What?"

I lower my arm onto the Bel Air windowsill and drum my fingers. "Well, you know my dad. He and I don't always get along, but at least he's real. My stepfather, I watch him talk to other people, and he's always trying to butter them up, crack stupid jokes, figure out their strengths and weaknesses."

"You mean like a politician?"

"Kind of. One who'll stab you in the back when you're not looking. He's always trying to give me advice about what I should do and how I should think. If I do something he doesn't like and my mom's not around, he blows up at me. Then when my mom's there, he smiles good-naturedly as if nothing just happened."

"Sounds like a jerk."

And a bully, I realize for the first time.

"I try not to even talk to him anymore," I continue. "You're lucky you're on your own."

As soon as I say it, I regret it. I think about Kyle's mom dying and Annie being forced to move. "I'm sorry," I tell him. "I didn't mean that."

But Kyle cuts me some slack. He lights his cigarette and observes, "It sounds like you don't fit in anywhere anymore."

I nod. "Yeah. That's about right."

FIVE

Interstate 65 is apparently not high on the Department of Transportation's priority list for our nation's new freeway system. After following the highway north from Montgomery, the road peters out, and we have to endure several miles of stoplights before the new freeway magically reappears again through the heart of downtown Birmingham.

As we finally enter the city, I can see that Birmingham is at least twice the size of Pensacola, but all I really know about the place is that it was important during the Civil Rights movement. Martin Luther King marched here, I think, and I remember seeing pictures of white policemen with barking dogs attacking black protestors. Or was that in Montgomery? I can't remember.

"Annie says they make a lot of iron and steel here," Kyle informs me. "Used to be called the Pittsburgh of the South."

"Huh," I say, interested. Smokestacks and brick buildings rise on either side of us, and it's not too hard imagining what the city might have been like a century ago.

Kyle pulls off the freeway, and takes me to a place he knows about called Constantine's, not far from the campus of Birmingham Southern College. The food is good and cheap, and I have to admit I don't mind the company of the college co-eds around me, either.

"Nice view, huh?" Kyle asks, catching me admiring the long, tanned legs of three college girls sitting at the table next to us.

My eyes snap back toward him and my face reddens. "Uh, yeah."

He laughs, and says, "We'd better get dessert, too, dontcha think?"

After lingering over thick slices of lemon pie and re-filling our Cokes, we finally drag ourselves away from the college girls, and drive to a suburb just north of the city.

"This is where your aunt lives?" I ask. "You ever been here before?"

"Just once," Kyle tells me, pulling off the exit.

I look over, and am surprised to see his brow furrowed, his knuckles white on the steering wheel. Ten minutes later, we rumble toward a blue, single-story, clapboard house with green wooden shutters. Kyle pulls over about fifty yards away and kills the engine.

"That your aunt's place?" I say, sucking on my Coke from Constantine's.

Kyle nods.

"Why didn't you stop in front of the house?"

"Well, they're not exactly expectin' us."

I pull the straw out of my mouth. "They're not? Didn't you call them?"

Kyle shakes his head. "My aunt and uncle and me, we're not sailin' the smoothest waters right now."

I process this new information.

"Is it because of Annie?"

"Yeah. When I was tryin' to keep Annie in Tampa, we all traded words a few times."

"They thought Annie should live with them?"

"Yeah," Kyle says, but doesn't elaborate.

This revelation surprises me, but I don't really worry about it. I trust Kyle and know what dealing with a screwed-up family can be like. Instead, I ask, "So what's the plan?"

"Let's wait here for a few minutes."

Kyle lights a cigarette and offers me one.

I shake my head. "You ought to quit those things."

He grunts. "I think it's too late. If I don't smoke one for an hour or so, I start feeling jumpy."

"Well, that's only going to get worse."

"Probably."

"I'm not trying to preach to you or anything," I tell him. "It's just I've watched my dad try to quit for years."

Kyle looks at me. "He's tried? How'd that go?"

"It didn't. Longest he lasted was about a day. I'm afraid he's going to get lung cancer."

Kyle flinches a little, and I'm guessing he's thinking about his mom. Then, he stubs out the cigarette against the outside of his door. "Okay, Mike. You win. From now on, I quit."

He turns to me and grins. "I knew there was a reason I stopped by Pensacola."

I don't really expect him to quit, but I laugh, relieved he's not mad at me. Then, I point up the street. "Hey, that's not Annie, is it?"

Kyle's eyes jerk toward the front windshield, and he quickly opens his door. "Stay here, okay?"

I watch as he jogs up the street. Annie walks by herself from the opposite direction, but even from a distance I can tell she's not the same tomboy I knew on Shipwreck Island. She's at least six inches taller, for one thing, and her little-girl figure has taken on quite a few new curves. When Kyle waves, she halts, and even from a hundred yards away, I see the gleam of her smile as she rushes toward him.

I feel a little self-conscious watching them embrace, but don't look away. I can't hear them talking, but can tell that Annie is elated to see her brother. Then, suddenly, their body language changes. Kyle stiffens and reaches for Annie's left cheek. She shakes her head, but he quickly starts toward his aunt's and uncle's house. Annie grabs him by the bicep, stopping him. It looks like she's pleading with him and at first, he resists. Then, he gives in. Annie hugs him again and rushes toward the house alone. Kyle returns to the car.

"What's happening?" I ask.

"We're going to take Annie out for a while. Okay with you?" Kyle's voice is grim, but I sense it's not the best time to ask questions.

"Sure," I say. "That's why we're here."

Five minutes later, Annie emerges from the house and carefully closes the door behind her. As she hurries toward our car, I notice she is carrying a large cloth bag.

Kyle starts the car, and I flop over into the back seat.

Annie rushes around to the passenger side, tosses in her bag, and climbs in after it, breathing heavily. "Let's go!"

The Bel Air lurches forward and we zoom past Kyle's aunt's house. I look at Kyle and Annie staring woodenly out the front windshield.

And for the first time, I get an uneasy feeling. A feeling that maybe this trip isn't quite what I thought it was going to be.

SIX

W e ride in silence for a few minutes. The hot afternoon air rushing through the windows feels
like it's blowing straight off of Birmingham's famous blast
furnaces. As we pull onto a two-lane highway on the east
side of the city, Annie finally turns to me.

"So how ya doin', Mike?"

Up-close, I get my first good look at Annie, and can
tell that she's changed in more ways than I first realized.
Her blonde hair is longer, and I notice a couple of zits on
her chin and next to her ear. She's lost her baby fat, that's
for sure. Mostly, though, it's her gaze that is different. Annie was always quiet and serious, but her blue eyes hold
something new now. I'm not sure what it is, and can't decide if it's good or bad, but I smile and answer her.

"Pretty good. It's nice to see you again."

Annie regards me for a moment, then says, "Yeah,
you too."

Before she turns back around, however, I glimpse
something else about her. A light greenish mark on her left
cheek. I'm not sure what it is, but remember Kyle touch-
ing her face a few minutes ago, and store the information
in my brain.

"So where are we going?" I ask Kyle.

He glances at me in his rearview mirror. "Just for a
drive out in the country. You hungry?" he asks Annie.

"I'm always hungry."

Kyle laughs. "Big surprise. I don't know how you stay
so skinny."

"Tapeworm," she replies.

"Well, we'll get something pretty soon."

Annie's and Kyle's shoulders relax more with every passing mile. As it becomes clear that we're leaving Birmingham, however, my own shoulders start to knot up.

"Kyle," I say. "We're heading back south. Do you know where you're going?"

Annie throws a sharp glance at her brother. "You didn't tell him?"

"Tell me what?"

Kyle looks back at Annie. "I wasn't sure how it was goin' to play out."

"Tell me what?" I repeat, leaning forward, gripping the back of the front bench seat.

Annie looks at me, then back at her brother. "Kyle, you gotta tell him."

Kyle sighs, then twists around toward me. "Uh, Mike."

"What?"

"Don't get mad or nothin', but Annie's not goin' back to Birmingham."

His words don't fully register. "What do you mean she's not going back?"

"We're not goin' back. Annie's comin' with me. I mean us."

"Coming where? Where are we going?"

"Well, I'm not exactly sure about that," he says. "We just ain't goin' back *there*."

I have no idea how to respond to this. I continue clutching the front seat, feeling dazed. Then, as I recover my wits, my grip on the seat grows tighter.

"Kyle!" I blurt. "Pull over!"

Kyle finds a wide space next to the road, and brings the Bel Air to a halt.

"Let me out," I say.

Annie gets out and flips her side of the front seat forward. As I hurl myself out into the Alabama heat and walk away from the car, I hear Kyle's door also open and his footsteps follow me.

"Mike..."

I wheel on him, and shout, "What are you **doing?**"

I expect Kyle to shout back at me, but his jaws stay clamped together.

"Don't you know this is *kidnapping?*" I continue. "You can't just take someone—even your sister—and drive away with her."

Kyle shoves his hands in his pockets. "I know."

"It's only going to be, what, a day, two days at most before the cops find you—find *us*—and throw us all in jail!"

"I was plannin' to drive you home like I said."

"That's not the point! The point is if you don't take Annie back—and soon—you're going to be in a lot of trouble. And you're going to get Annie in trouble, too."

By now, Annie has walked over to a magnolia tree, giving us space.

"You don't understand," Kyle tells me.

"No, I don't understand. You made it sound like we were just going to take a little road trip. Like Jack Kerouac or something. Instead, all you wanted me for was an accomplice."

"It ain't like that," Kyle says, fishing around for a cigarette. "I coulda done this by myself. I just thought it would be fun to see you again. Catch up on things."

I can tell Kyle is speaking the truth, and that lets some of the steam out from under my hood. I kick at a clump of red clay.

"Okay, so we've caught up. Now, you've got to take Annie back home, and drive me back to Pensacola."

Kyle finds his pack of cigarettes and lights one up. He inhales deeply and lets out a blue cloud big enough to kill every mosquito in a half-mile radius.

"Can't do it."

"Okay, then just put me on a bus," I say. "My dad gave me enough money for a ticket."

"No, I mean I can't take Annie back."

"Are you crazy? Didn't you hear the part about getting thrown in jail?"

"You don't understand," he says again.

"*What* don't I understand?"

Kyle takes another drag on his cigarette and then drops it into the dirt. He stares down at it as he grinds it into shreds with the toe of his shoe. Finally, he casts a quick glance at Annie and looks me in the eyes.

"It's my uncle," he tells me. "He's layin' into Annie."

SEVEN

"What do you mean he's layin' into her?" But before I even finish the sentence, a chunk of lead drops into my stomach.

Annie is still over by the magnolia tree, and Kyle nods toward her. "You see that bruise on her face?"

"Your uncle did that? No. You're kidding."

"Wish I was."

I've heard of child abuse before, but this is the first time I've ever come face to face with it. A kind of disbelief spreads through me.

"That's not all," Kyle tells me, and the lead in my gut grows heavier. "Annie said he locked her in the closet once to punish her."

I shake my head. "Are you serious? For how long?"

"I don't know, but my dad—my *real* dad, not Ray— used to beat my mom all the time. I remember seein' it. Each time it happened it got worse 'til finally she ended up in the hospital. I was too young to stop it then, but I ain't now. If I didn't come get Annie, it was going to get bad. Real bad."

A drop of sweat rolls into my left eye and I try to wipe away the sting.

"Does your aunt know?"

Kyle shrugs. "About the beating? Probably. But my uncle's in charge. Probably not a whole lot she can do about it. He probably hits her, too."

"*What?* Can't you tell somebody?"

Kyle's eyes grow harder. "Who, Mike? Who's gonna

believe me?"

I don't have an answer for that.

"Look," he tells me, his voice a growl. "I've a mind to take care of my uncle myself. Just one swing of a lug wrench and it'd be all over. But then I'd be in jail for sure and Annie wouldn't have nobody."

Despite the oppressive heat, a shudder ripples through me. As I stare at Kyle, I have no doubt he'd do just what he's saying he would.

"But Kyle," I say. "You're going to end up in jail *this* way, don't you see?"

"At least this way, we got a chance."

Not much of one, I think.

"C'mon," Kyle tells me. "I'll take you to the bus station."

I don't move. "Who said I want to go to the bus station?"

"You did. I already told you I'm not takin' Annie back. And they'll be lookin' for us if we go back to Florida. You don't want to be mixed up in a man-hunt, do you?"

"Well..." Suddenly, I am not sure what I want. I like Kyle and Annie, but as awful as it is, this isn't really my fight. Then again, I've got a terrible feeling about what they're doing.

Another drop of sweat stings my eye.

"So?" Kyle asks.

I can almost hear my brain cells sizzling from the sun blasting down through my head. I want to think this all through more carefully, but the late afternoon rays seem to paralyze my thought processes.

"Okay. Take me to the bus," I say, and start walking back toward the Bel Air.

As Kyle and I get in the car, Annie is already sitting in the back seat. "You tell him?" she asks her brother.

Kyle nods.

"Everything?"

Kyle turns the ignition key and the Bel Air roars to life. "I had to, Annie."

"I told you not to tell him everything."

"He's a friend. He won't tell anyone."

Annie's voice breaks. "Darn you, Kyle." I don't turn around to look at her, but can hear her sniffling in the back seat.

None of us say anything on the drive back into Birmingham. What started as a fun adventure has turned into something, well, something I don't even want to think about. I'm not just upset for myself. I'm also worried about Kyle and Annie. As we drive, I play out different scenarios for what might happen to them, but none of them end up good. Half an hour later, after a stop to ask directions, Kyle pulls up to a curb in the heart of the city. Just down the block, the late evening rays of the sun strike a two-story-high sign reading "GREYHOUND".

"This is it," Kyle says. "C'mon. I'll walk you in. You come with us, Annie."

"I'm stayin' here."

"Annie, don't give me that. It might not be safe."

I glance around and see that the area doesn't look too bad. Most Greyhound stations I've seen are surrounded by liquor stores and bail bondsmen. Here, all I see are government buildings. Still, I'd also feel better if Annie came in with us.

She wants none of it.

"I'm stayin'!" she repeats in no uncertain terms.

"Well, at least lock the doors after us."

She pouts and doesn't reply.

I grab my AWOL bag. "Bye, Annie."

"Bye," she mutters without looking at me. Kyle and I walk down to the station.

I've never actually been inside a Greyhound station, but as we walk through the doors, it's the smell that hits me first—a combination of cigarette smoke, greasy food, and bathroom cleaning supplies.

Kyle and I head to the ticket window and I ask when the next bus leaves for Pensacola.

"Next bus for Mobile's at ten o'clock," the woman tells me. "From there, you change buses. You'll get into Pensacola at 5:45 a.m."

I look up at the clock behind the woman.

7:50 p.m., I think to myself. *It's going to be a long night.*

"Okay. One ticket, please."

"That'll be eleven dollars."

I hand her one of the twenty-dollar bills my dad gave me, and she counts out the change. I shove it into my pocket with the ticket, and Kyle and I move away from the window.

"You want us to wait with you?" Kyle asks. "We can all go get a bite to eat."

I scan the bus station. It is not a happy place. Several people are slumped over in uncomfortable chairs, trying to sleep. A couple of young guys not much older than I am study the passengers with sharp eyes. I can only guess what they are thinking.

I begin counting my teeth with my tongue—something I do when I'm nervous. "No," I tell Kyle. "You two better get moving."

Kyle also studies the depot. "You sure, Mike?"

I turn to face him. "Kyle, what's your plan, anyway? Where are you going to go?"

Kyle takes a deep breath and I can tell the full impact of his actions is just starting to sink in. He runs his hand through his shock of dark-blonde hair. "To tell ya the truth, I don't rightly know. All I know is that as soon as I got Annie's letter, I had to get up here fast."

We stand there for another minute. My brain is working overtime and I want to say something, but I just don't know what. Before I can figure it out, Kyle sticks out his hand. "Well, Mike. I'm sorry I got you into this."

I stare at his hand, then stick out my own. "Don't worry about it."

"Okay, then. I'll be seein' you."

Kyle starts to turn away.

"Wait," I tell him.

I reach into my pocket for the rest of my cash and hand it to him. Kyle waves it away.

"Naw, man. I can't take that."

I seize his hand and press the bills into it. "Really. Take it. You're going to need it."

Kyle looks down at the money for a moment, then nods.

"I'll pay you back."

"You'd better."

He lets out a half-laugh. Then, we shake hands again before I watch him walk out of the station.

EIGHT

I try to select a seat away from other people, but the station is crowded enough that I don't have a lot of choices. Going for the lesser of evils, I sit one chair away from a snoring, grizzled man wrapped in a stained Army jacket. His fingers curl around a brown paper bag with a clear glass neck periscoping out of it. As soon as I sit, I realize why the seats next to him are empty. Each time he exhales, a chemical cloud of fumes washes over me. I have no idea what napalm smells like, but this could be pretty close.

Across from me sits an older black woman reading a Bible. Catching my glance, she smiles. "Is the only place he can sleep safe 'round here," she says, nodding to the man. "Is a cold-hearted shame how they treat these men comin' home from the war."

I ponder the snoring Vietnam veteran, feeling sorry for him. Part of me also feels guilty—and glad—that I was too young to get drafted into the war myself. Thinking about Vietnam, though, makes me remember the article about the mysterious silver dollars that were minted and melted right when the war was starting to get big.

I'm not really in a reading mood, but I've got a lot of time to kill, and I need something to get my mind off of Kyle and Annie. I reach into my AWOL bag and pull out my copy of the *Coin Universe*, and flip to page four. "Ah," I whisper, and pick up reading where I had left off:

The new silver dollar proposal proved unpopular from the start. After the elimination of silver from United States dimes and quarters in 1965, older silver coins were already being hoarded in huge numbers by coin collectors across the nation. This led to a national shortage of coins for commerce. Treasury officials and members of Congress had no doubt that the new proposed silver dollars would also be grabbed up as soon as they were released.

That didn't stop Senate Majority Leader Mike Mansfield (D-Montana) from pushing both Treasury officials and President Lyndon B. Johnson to quietly proceed with the plan. Between May 13th and May 24th, 1965, two coin presses at the Mint's Denver facility produced approximately 322,000 silver dollars with the Peace dollar design on them. Even though they were being minted in 1965, the dollars were all dated 1964 and carried a 'D' mintmark to denote the Denver Mint.

When news of the new silver dollars reached Washington, it unleashed a firestorm of opposition. Members of Congress demanded an immediate halt to the program, and on May 25th, 1965, the program was terminated. Shortly thereafter, the new silver dollars were melted, and for years afterward, the Mint denied they had ever had existed.

I finish the story and think to myself, *Wow. Wouldn't it be cool to find one of those Peace dollars?*

My thoughts return to the Confederate double eagles Kyle and I discovered on Shipwreck Island, and I can't help smiling remembering what we went through to get them. As I think about Kyle, though, my smile fades and I again start worrying about him and Annie. Part of me thinks I should do something—anything—to help. Another part of me warns that it's none of my business. I tap my heel. I look all around the bus station. So many conflicting thoughts and feelings whirl through me that a balloon of anxiety rises in my chest.

Finally, I pick up my AWOL bag and carry it to a bank of payphones on the nearby wall. A girl a little older than I am is sobbing into one of the phones, so I choose a phone at the opposite end of the row, pick up the receiver, and dial '0'.

The line rings once before a woman's voice answers. "Operator. What city please?"

"Pensacola."

"One moment please."

The first operator transfers me to a second operator, who asks, "May I help you?"

"I'd like to make a collect call."

I recite the number and my name, and a few moments later, the line is ringing. I hear my father's voice pick up. "Hello?"

The operator tells him, "I have a collect call from Mike Gilbert. Will you accept the charges?"

"Yes."

"Thank you."

"Son, are you okay?" my dad asks, unable to keep the worry from his voice.

"I'm fine," I say.

"Where are you? What are you doing?"

"Well, uh, Kyle and I made it to Birmingham."

"Did you find Annie?"

"Yeah."

"How's she doing?"

"She's all grown up," I tell him.

He laughs. "I'll bet."

When I first picked up the phone, I had intended to tell my dad the truth about Kyle and Annie, to see if he had any ideas for how to help them. I've always been able to talk to my father, and usually, he's given me good advice. Now, though, I hesitate. Part of it is that he's hundreds of miles away. *Too far away to help*, I think. But I also hear screaming on the other end of the phone line. "Uh, is everything alright back there?" I ask.

"Well, you can probably hear," my dad admits. "David's got a 102-degree temperature."

"Is that serious?"

"Naw. Just some baby crud. But he's not real happy about things, and Paula and I have spent the whole day taking turns holding him."

I hear Paula shout something.

"It's Mike," my dad shouts back at her.

"So, uh," he says, "You're in Birmingham."

"That's right."

"How long you going to stay?"

I pull out my bus ticket and stare down at it. "I'm—"

"What? I can't hear you."

And suddenly, I make a decision.

Instead of giving him my bus schedule, I ask, "Um, is it all right if I stay another couple of days?"

He pauses, and I can hear David wailing even louder in the background.

My dad says, "Well, we miss you, son. But like I said, things aren't much fun around here at the moment. Sure, go ahead. Just give me a heads up when you're going to be back."

"Are you sure?" Already, I can feel guilt tugging at me.

"You and Kyle go have some fun," he repeats. "We'll all be waiting for you."

"Okay. Thanks."

I hang up the receiver, seize my AWOL bag, and rush out of the station.

▼

NINE

Even though I couldn't have been in the station more than fifteen minutes, I know it's a long shot that I'll find Kyle and Annie. *By now, they're probably halfway to Memphis—or wherever they decided to go,* I tell myself. I almost think I'm imagining it when I see the Bel Air still sitting in its same spot. Just to make sure I'm not hallucinating, I walk up to the window and peer in. Sure enough, two empty cups from Constantine's sit on the floor where Kyle and I left them earlier.

"But where are Kyle and Annie?" I mutter, straightening up and leaning back against the car.

Then, I hear a familiar voice. "Mike!"

I spin around to see Kyle and Annie crossing the street.

"What happened?" he asks as they step up onto the sidewalk. "You forget somethin'?"

"Where were you?" I ask, relieved to see them.

Kyle motions to a corner store down the street. "Annie forgot to bring a couple a things. Toothpaste and stuff."

"Did you decide where you're going?"

Kyle looks over at Annie. "Well, Annie said she's always wanted to see Chicago. We got another aunt up there, so we thought that'd be our best bet."

Annie is just staring down at the sidewalk, but I tell Kyle. "Well, I might have a better idea."

Annie's eyes lift up to me, and Kyle asks, "What?"

Even though the sun has gone down, waves of heat still boil up off of the cement. I wipe sweat off of my forehead. "Let's go somewhere cooler to talk about it."

Twenty minutes later, we are sitting crammed together in a narrow Waffle House booth north of Birmingham.

After we order, Kyle asks, "So, what's this plan of yours?"

"Well, I haven't thought it out completely," I say, opening up the copy of the *Coin Universe* newspaper I've brought into the restaurant with me. I turn to page four, point to the article on the 1964 Peace Dollar, and hand it to Kyle. Kyle brushes a strand of hair from his eyes and reads through it. Finally, he returns the paper and says, "I'm not gettin' ya, Mike. What's this got to do with us?"

"Maybe nothing," I admit. "But maybe something, too. In the article, it says they minted more than a quarter million of these Peace dollars."

"And then melted 'em down afterward," Kyle says. "Because Congress thought it was a dumb idea. So?"

Annie finally decides to enter the conversation. "What's a Peace dollar?"

I show her the photo that goes along with the article. "It's the last kind of silver dollar the U.S. government ever made—unless you count the Eisenhower dollars, which I *don't*. Anyway, this article says that in 1965, after thirty years of not making silver dollars, the government decided to make a whole bunch more. And then, supposedly, they melted them all down."

Annie's gaze starts to drift, and I can tell I'm losing her.

Kyle cuts back in. "Mike, what do you mean they *supposedly* melted 'em down? It says right here that they *did* melt 'em down."

I shift my eyes from Annie back to Kyle—and have

to admit I'm a bit reluctant to do so. For the first time I'm realizing that Annie hasn't just grown up. Underneath her sloppy hair and scattering of zits, she's become more than a little beautiful, with full lips, and a slender face and neck—not to mention her brother's penetrating blue eyes.

"Mike?" Kyle prompts me.

"Oh, yeah." I take a deep breath and explain. "Kyle, if you worked at the U.S. Mint, and you'd just made the only new silver dollars in the past thirty years, don't you think you'd at least consider keeping one? Even as a souvenir?"

Kyle picks up a little white sugar packet and starts turning it over in his fingers. "Okay, Mike. Yeah, I can see what you're sayin', but the Mint ain't gonna just let anyone walk out with one 'a those coins."

"No. But Kyle, there were three hundred and twenty-two *thousand* of them. You think the Mint counted every single one when they melted them? What's more," I press on, "do you know how much a rich collector would pay to get ahold of one of them?"

"Then or now?"

"Now," I say, but Kyle has brought up a good point. Back when they were minting them, no one knew these silver dollars might turn into rare coins.

"But," I continue. "Even then, before they all got melted down, a collector or dealer might pay something to be first to get one of the coins. Maybe even enough money to convince a Mint employee to sneak a few of them out of the Mint. If they did, it means a few of the coins could have survived."

Kyle shrugs. "Sounds like a long shot, but I s'pose it's possible."

Annie again darts back to the conversation. "You sayin' these silver dollars are worth a lot of money?"

"Annie," Kyle says. "These things don't even exist."

"Maybe they do," I counter.

We have to suspend our conversation when the waitress arrives. Even though it's dinnertime, I've ordered a cheese omelette and hash browns, and I don't wait to begin shoveling them into my mouth with large, ravenous bites. Annie and Kyle have gone for cheeseburgers and attack them with equal gusto. After finishing half his meal, Kyle again speaks.

"So what're you saying, Mike? You sayin' Annie and me should go *find* one of these Peace dollars? Just drive on out to Denver and start askin' around?"

Hearing him say it out loud makes me realize what a far-fetched idea it is. On the other hand, it's not any worse than what Kyle and Annie have thought up by themselves today. If Kyle and Annie plan to be on the run and find new lives for themselves, they're going to need a chunk of cash. A 1964 Peace dollar could give it to them.

"Why not?" I ask him. "What have we got to lose? You and me, well…"

I pause and glance pointedly at Annie, wondering if Kyle has told her about the double eagles. Kyle gives me a slight shake of his head. "You and me," I say, choosing my words carefully, "it's not like we don't have some *experience* with this kind of thing."

My tone of voice does not escape Annie. She takes a sip of her soft drink and eyes me curiously. "What do y'all mean?"

"I, uh, mean, we've both collected coins some, and kind of know what we're looking for."

Annie punches her brother in the shoulder. "When

have you done any coin collectin'? You just have them little books with pennies and nickels under your bed."

Before Kyle can answer, I cut in, lowering my voice. "Look, maybe finding a 1964 Peace Dollar is a crazy idea. But going to Denver is smart. No one will be looking for us there. They'll expect us to go back to Florida, or somewhere else in the South. And really, Chicago? Kyle, if you've got relatives there, that's the first place they'll look for you."

Kyle doesn't say anything, but I can see the calculations behind his eyes.

"If we're really going to do this," I continue, "we've got to get a step ahead of them."

Kyle takes another bite of his burger and chews thoughtfully. Then, he says, "You keep sayin' 'we', Mike. You plannin' to come with us?"

I hedge. "I, uh…maybe for a couple of days."

"What about your dad? He gonna let you do that?"

"I already called him. He's okay with it."

Sort of.

Kyle shakes his head. "I don' know, Mike. Like you said, they catch us, we're all in a lot of trouble. You too. I was stupid for askin' you to come in the first place. I don' want to risk something happenin' to you."

I eat the last bit of my omelette and swallow. "Look," I say, "to tell you the truth, I don't want to go back to Pensacola. Not yet. David's sick and…I'm just not ready to go back."

I turn my eyes to Annie. "What about you? Is it all right if I come?"

Annie sticks a fry in her mouth and twirls it like a toothpick. She glances at her brother, then back to me.

"Kyle always said you were cool, so yeah. I guess it's alright."

"Kyle?" I ask.

He wipes his mouth and wads up his napkin. He looks over at the Waffle House cook, who is flipping a couple of eggs in a pan. Then, he tells me, "Mike, you know I want you to come along, but I don't know about this Denver thing. I still think we'd be better off goin' to Chicago. If we do that, you still want to come?"

I take a long drink of water, thinking. Then, I set my glass down. "Okay. Forget Denver. Let's go to Chicago."

TEN

When we get back to the Bel Air, I take the front passenger seat and Annie sits in back.

"How much money do we have altogether?" I ask, as I buckle my seatbelt.

The Bel Air roars to life and Kyle shoves the stick into reverse. "Including what you gave me? Prob'ly about a hundred and twenty bucks."

"We—you—could use more."

"Well," he says, burning out of the Waffle House parking lot. "I got me an idea about that."

Kyle continues north out of town, following two-lane roads. Half an hour later, we cruise into a little burg called Oneonta. We rumble through a quaint Main Street, then Kyle says, "We gotta get some gas."

We pull into a Gulf filling station and are approached by an attendant who has the name "DJ" stitched on his blue uniform. He looks even younger than we are.

"Five gallons 'a Regular," Kyle tells him.

"Don't you want to just fill it up?" I ask. "We're going to need it anyway."

Kyle gives me a sly grin. "No, we won't. Not yet."

The attendant—DJ—stops pumping, and says, "That'll be $2.20 total."

Kyle whistles. "I sure hope gas comes down again soon. These prices are killin' me."

He hands the attendant a five dollar bill, and while the kid is counting out change, asks him, "So, DJ. You know a place around here called Blackwell Bottoms?"

Annie suddenly scoots forward in the back seat.

DJ stops counting money and looks at Kyle. Then, he runs his eyes all along the body of the Bel Air. With a lowered voice, he asks, "Y'all plannin' to do some racin'?"

I almost blurt out *What?*, but catch myself.

Kyle shrugs. "Just thought we'd check out the local action."

DJ again studies our car. "There's some mighty fast boys out there. Two of 'em got Chevelles. One's got a 396. The other has a 454."

"We'll be careful," Kyle assures him.

DJ gives Kyle directions to Blackwell Bottoms while continuing to inspect the Bel Air.

Kyle thanks him and says, "And DJ? My change?"

"Oh, uh, yeah."

DJ thrusts the money at Kyle and the Bel Air again fires up. As Kyle puts the stick into first gear, DJ says, "I sure hope y'all know what you're doin'."

Leaving Oneonta, we head west, over a hill, through dark woods and farms. After a few miles, we come to a crossroads and turn north.

"Kyle, what's this all about?" I ask. "What the heck is Blackwell Bottoms?"

"One of the guys that brings his car into the shop down in Tampa told me about it," Kyle explains. "When I'm workin', lotsa guys come in to shoot the bull. They know I'm into racin' so we swap stories. This one guy's from up here somewhere. He told me to look up this place called Blackwell Bottoms where all the local motor heads go."

Annie's hanging over the front seat between us now,

her face close and smiling. "I knew you was up to somethin'. You think you can take these guys?"

"Wait," I say. "You're not really going to race, are you? I don't know much about cars, but isn't a 454 a huge engine?"

Kyle nods seriously, like a professor considering an academic problem. "It is," he says, but before he can say more, we enter a flat, straight stretch of road and see a couple of dozen cars and pickup trucks scattered along the pavement ahead. Kyle downshifts and eases the Bel Air right into the center of things.

All eyes turn to us as Kyle pulls over and parks half off the pavement. By the time we're out of the car, a crowd surrounds us.

"How y'all doin'?" Kyle says, flashing his signature grin. While I start counting my teeth, Kyle's voice stays steady, confident.

"Doin' pretty fine," one guy answers. He's wearing a NASCAR cap and looks to be in his mid- to late twenties. "Watcha got in that '57 there?"

Kyle walks around to the front of the Bel Air. "Take a look," he tells them, popping the hood.

Everyone crowds around the engine. Portable electric lights have been set up and they cast plenty of glare over the Bel Air and the crowd. While everyone starts talking about Kyle's car, I study my surroundings more closely. I count at least sixty, maybe seventy-five people milling around. Not just guys, either. More than a few girlfriends have shown up. Many of the people grip cans of beer and soda, and I even catch the whiff of hamburgers barbequing somewhere. I also notice another strong odor in the air.

"What's that smell?" I ask a cute girl wearing jeans

and a baseball cap.

She points to a bank of lights several hundred yards across a field. "Chicken factory," she says. "You'll get used to it."

Then, I hear a guy ask Kyle, "Where'd you get that 454?"

"Wrecked Corvette," he tells the guy. "Swung a trade for it."

I elbow Annie. "Kyle told me he put a big block engine in the Bel Air—not a 454."

She laughs. "You don't know much about cars, do ya Mike? A 454 is the biggest big block engine you can get."

"That a Holley 780?" someone else asks Kyle.

I again nudge Annie. "What's a Holley?"

"The carburetor."

"Yep," Kyle answers. "'Course, I had to put in some traction bars to keep the whole thing steady."

The other gearheads nod knowingly. Then, a guy with greasy black hair and a Lynyrd Skynyrd T-shirt steps forward and asks, "So, y'all here to cackle or race?"

Kyle regards him as if he's evaluating a ball-peen hammer. "Depends on what you got in mind."

People have stepped back to give Mr. Skynyrd some room, and he points over to an orange Chevelle with the chrome insignia SS 396 on the side.

Kyle glances at it, then back at Mr. Skynyrd. "Well, seein' as how I'm a newcomer here, I don't want to embarrass nobody."

"Ooooh!" some of the girlfriends say, and I hear more than a few chuckles from the guys.

Kyle continues to bait the guy. "You sure you want to take me on in that lil 'ole thing?"

I whisper to Annie. "Can Kyle beat him?"

Annie whispers back, "Well, the Chevelle's got the smaller engine, but it depends on what else his owner might 'a done to it. I seen 396s beat 454s before."

Even under the artificial lights, I notice that Mr. Skynyrd's face has definitely turned a shade of pink.

"You callin' me out, boy?"

Kyle splays his palms apologetically. "No, sir. Course not. I just mean, well, you see what I got under the hood."

"It's one thing to talk big," Skynyrd says. "It's another to put some money on it."

More oohs and clucking from the crowd.

Kyle scratches his cheek. "What're ya thinkin'?"

"Twenty bucks."

Kyle considers this. "Forty's got a smoother sound to it."

The girl I talked to earlier says to me, "Your friend better watch out. That orange Chevelle's the second-fastest thing out here."

"What's the fastest?" I ask.

Before she can answer, Kyle says to Mr. Skynyrd. "Tell you what. Since I got the bigger engine, I'll even carry my friend with me, add a little more weight to the front. Slow us down a little."

"Wha—?" As Kyle points toward me, visions of a hundred-mile-per-hour rolling fireball fill my head.

Annie puts her hand on my bicep. "Don't worry, Mike. I've raced with Kyle before. He don't usually mess up."

Usually? I think, but I also realize I like her hand resting on my arm.

"Look," Kyle tells the orange Chevelle owner. "If

you're really worried about it, I'll even give you a fifty-yard head start."

That does it. The gauntlet has been thrown.

"You're on!" Skynyrd shouts. "And I don' need no head start to take you, neither!"

ELEVEN

66 "Kyle, why are we doing this?"

I am sitting in the passenger seat of the Bel Air, Kyle at the wheel.

"Better strap in," Kyle tells me, but my seatbelt is already cinched tight enough to prevent my Waffle House dinner from ever reaching my small intestine.

Kyle puts the car into first gear. Someone has poured a shallow pool of water onto the roadway, and Kyle eases into it. Then he places one foot on the brake and with the other, presses down on the gas. Immediately, the roar of the big block engine fills my ears and I feel the shudder of the back wheels spinning on the wet pavement. His foot still on the brake, Kyle lets them spin for about five seconds, the car jitterbugging forward until it pops out onto dry pavement.

I cough at the cloud of vaporized rubber filling the Bel Air's interior.

"What are you *doing?*"

"Just roastin' the meat," Kyle says, business-like. "Warmin' up the tires. They grip better that way."

All around us, people are whooping and cheering at the spectacle. Next to us, the Chevelle also vaporizes some perfectly good tire tread, and an even bigger cheer goes up.

Both drivers inch their cars up to a foot-wide white line painted across the road. Kyle and I look over at Mr. Skynyrd, and he glares back at us and loudly revs his engine.

Kyle revs his back.

"Kyle," I say. "This is nuts. You're going to kill both of us. And why do I have to come along with you? Will it really slow you down?"

"Maybe a bit." Kyle doesn't take his eyes off of Mr. Skynyrd, but his voice is relaxed. Confident. "Mostly, I just thought you might enjoy it, Mike. You seemed to like to go fast before."

"Fast, yeah. But this? *This?*"

The guy with the NASCAR cap steps between the vehicles and shouts, "It's a quarter-mile race gentlemen, to the white finish line yonder."

I look down the road to see another group of people gathered next to the road a quarter mile away.

"Winner takes all—$80," he says, waving the money in his hand. "Loser gets squat. Keep it clean. We don't want anyone gettin' hurt out here tonight. Understood?"

Kyle revs the Bel Air and flashes an "O.K." sign.

All around me, I see other money changing hands. *Side bets.*

I don't spot Annie anywhere, but before I can give that much thought, the NASCAR guy takes up a position even with the front bumpers, right between the Bel Air and the Chevelle.

"You boys ready?"

Both Kyle and Mr. Skynyrd nod.

NASCAR raises the $80 bet above his head.

"On the count of three. One…Two…THREE!"

The man drops his hand, and the deafening roar of both engines pummels my ears. Kyle pops the clutch, and I slam back into my seat. And believe me, this is nothing like before. Now, I feel like I've just been shot out of a cannon. We bolt forward, engines screaming. It's all I can do to keep my head up and eyes looking forward.

Kyle accelerates until our engine sounds like it's going to explode, then in a flash, he shifts to the next gear. The Bel Air takes a quick breath, then accelerates even faster. Trees and shadows streak past me.

Even more insane whining from the engine and another shift.

I catch a glimpse of the orange Chevelle.

People's faces whip past.

And it's over.

Just like that.

"Did we win?" I shout, gasping, as Kyle eases off of the gas and downshifts. By the time I get the words out, we are already another quarter mile down the road.

Kyle casts me a quick grin. "By an elephant's trunk," he tells me.

"How fast were we going?"

Kyle slows to a stop and turns the Bel Air around. As he does, he checks the dashboard. I never noticed it before, but like everything else in the car, the speedometer is not standard. It's got an extra needle that is frozen up near the top end.

Kyle tells me, "According to this, we hit 119 miles per hour."

"Geez!"

He socks me in the shoulder. "Whaddya think? You like it?"

"Geez," I say again. "I don't...yeah! *Hell yeah!*"

I whoop loudly out of window.

Kyle throws back his head and laughs. "I knew ya would."

We drive slowly back past the finish line, and people holler at us and slap the Bel Air's trunk and hood. Kyle keeps rolling back to the starting line.

"Let's get our money and get out of here," I tell him.

Kyle doesn't even look at me. "Not so fast, Mike. We got one more race."

"*What?*"

He pulls the Bel Air over to the side of the road and shuts it off. Immediately, we are surrounded. Kyle climbs out and, still shaking with adrenaline, I follow.

A very unhappy man wearing a Lynyrd Skynyrd T-shirt approaches.

"You got lucky," he snarls.

Kyle doesn't take it personally. "Probably did," he says, coolly holding out his hand. "Thanks for givin' me a good race."

I can tell Mr. Skynyrd is looking for a reason to pick a fight, but Kyle isn't giving him one. With a growl, he shakes Kyle's hand and stalks away.

Mr. NASCAR comes up and hands Kyle the money. "Good race."

"Well," Kyle says, stuffing the money in his pocket. "Thanks for a lovely evenin'."

He turns back toward the Bel Air, when a smooth, deep voice asks, "What's the rush, Slick?"

Feigning surprise, Kyle turns back around. Making his way through the crowd is a towering, lean giant of a man with a military-style haircut and ebony skin. The crowd parts to give him room, and I see people whispering and nodding to each other.

Both Kyle and I have to look up to meet the man's eyes. It's not a comfortable feeling. The guy wears a dark green tank top and brownish camouflage cargo pants. His massive bicep displays a tattoo for the United States Marine Corps.

"What's your hurry?" the man repeats.

Kyle shrugs, and I wonder if his heart is beating as fast as mine. "No hurry. Just thought we'd run out of competition."

The man doesn't smile. He just points to a metallic purple demon with black racing stripes traveling the hood and roof, and says, "Not even close."

Kyle studies the car and whistles. "That a 1970 Chevelle, stock 454?"

"That, it is," the man replies. "And it likes to eat boys like you for a midnight snack."

Fresh hoots go up from the bystanders, and the cute girl I was talking to earlier shouts, "Give it to him, Jake!"

Kyle frowns. "I don' know, man. Don't seem like a fair fight. My car's a lot older 'n yours, and this is your home track."

The man—Jake—lets out a chuckle, but his eyes aren't smiling. "Don't be so modest, stranger. We got the same engines, right?"

"Well, yeah," Kyle answers.

Then, Jake steps close enough so only Kyle and I can hear him. He puts a hand on Kyle's shoulder and says, "And just between you and me? I think you'd go even faster if you weren't sandbagging this time."

Kyle's eyes flash briefly. "Got no idea what you're talkin' about."

Jake steps back and says, "I'll *bet* you don't. So, what do you say? Are we going to dance?"

Kyle again looks over at the '70 Chevelle. "How much?"

Jake asks, "How much you got?"

"Uh, I could maybe go forty again."

"I'm thinkin' a hundred."

"*One Hundred!*" Kyle whistles. "Too rich for my blood."

Jake's eyes don't waver. "Somehow, I doubt that."

Kyle slowly sweeps the hair out of his face. "You give me odds?"

Jake turns to the crowd. "What do you say, boys? Should I give this stranger odds?"

The "Yeah"s drown out the "No"s, and Jake says, "Okay. 2 to 1. I win, you hand me your $100. You win, I give up two C-notes."

Kyle sighs fretfully. "I think I'm gonna regret this."

TWELVE

K yle, Annie, and I walk back to the Bel Air.
"Kyle, can you really take this guy?" I ask.

"Sure hope so."

I grab his arm, forcing him to look at me. "What'd he mean by sandbagging?"

Kyle shrugs. "He just noticed I wasn't startin' in first gear."

My face remains a blank.

"I started in second gear," Kyle elaborates. "It sounds like you're drivin' all out, but because of the gear ratios, you're startin' out slower."

"Why would you want to do that?"

"To make it seem closer 'n it was," Annie joins in.

Slowly, the shades in my head are pulled back. "Wait. You mean, you *wanted* to set this race up as the underdog?"

Kyle slaps me on the shoulder. "You'll catch on, Big Mike."

We resume walking. "But," I say, like a coyote chewing a meaty bone. "This guy's fast, isn't he? You still think you can beat him?"

We reach the Bel Air, and Kyle turns to me again. "Honestly? Well, we'll find out in a couple 'a minutes."

"But Kyle. You're betting all of our money!"

"Had to, Mike, or he wouldn't 'a raced me."

He opens the driver's door, and I hurry around to the passenger side. As I reach for the handle, Kyle says, "Better sit this one out, Mike. I wanna run as light as possible."

My hand freezes. "Oh, right."

Kyle winks at me. "Keep your fingers crossed."

Annie and I watch as Kyle and the owner of the purple Chevelle start up their cars and take turns "roasting the meat" in the shallow pool of water on the pavement. Again, the vaporized rubber clouds send me into a coughing fit, and again, the bystanders meet every engine roar with even louder cheers. Excitement, like lightning, crackles through the crowd. It's the energy of the first race multiplied by two—or three or four or five. I can literally feel the electric charges dance up my arms and down my back.

"What do you think, Annie?"

Her face also glows with the moment, but her lips stay tight. "He's got a chance."

The purple Chevelle roars again.

I suddenly frown. "What do you mean, a chance? That's all? Have you ever seen Kyle beat someone like this before?"

Annie takes a deep breath. "Not in the Bel Air. But he'd just started rebuilding it when I had to move to Birmingham. I think it's all gonna come down to who's the better driver."

We watch as the two lions prowl up to the starting line. Mr. NASCAR again gives the drivers instructions and raises the $300 bet high above his head.

Suddenly, a sense of dread fills me. I want to close my eyes, but am riveted by the drama unfolding in front of me.

"Can't we stop this?" I ask Annie.

"Not now."

NASCAR shouts "Ready...Set..."

Annie slips her hand into mine.

"GO!"

NASCAR's arm flashes down and the two dragsters blast off.

The roar of the two mammoth engines sucks the oxygen from my lungs. As the two hot rods shoot off of the starting line, even I can tell that Kyle is going faster than before. His engine quickly whines up to ideal shifting speed, drops into second, and whines up again before quickly dropping into third. The purple Chevelle matches Kyle pulse for pulse, and the crowd swarms onto the roadway to watch from behind.

From the rear, I can't tell who is winning. The two muscle cars seem dead even as they sprint toward the finish. More engine whine. One final gear shift. Another thousand milliseconds and they are past the line, coasting to a halt almost a mile away.

Annie pries her hand out of mine, and I realize I must have been breaking her finger bones with my grip.

"Who won?" I shout.

Annie doesn't respond, but cocks her ear down the track. I don't hear anything, probably because the two dragsters have deafened me.

Then, slowly, Annie's mouth curves into a smile.

"We did!"

"How do you know?"

She nods toward the finish line. "No one's cheering at the other end!"

Twenty minutes later, our whoops and hollers shoot out across the dark, deserted Alabama countryside rushing by.

"We did it!" I yell, ignoring the fact that I had nothing to do with Kyle's victories tonight.

Annie pounds Kyle's shoulders from the back seat. "Great drivin', Brother."

Kyle is holding his left hand out the open window, feeling the damp nighttime breeze. He's not saying anything, but with the grin on his face, he doesn't have to.

"Tell the truth," I say. "Did you *know* you could beat him?"

Kyle ponders the question. "I knew if I drove me a solid race, I'd probably take him down."

"But how? His car is newer than yours. His engine is the same size as yours..."

Kyle looks pointedly back at Annie.

She blurts, "You *didn't*!"

I look blankly from one to the other. "Didn't what?"

Annie flings herself back in her seat and claps her hands together.

"I don't get it. What's the joke?" I say.

"Well, Mike," Kyle admits. "Our engines weren't *exactly* the same size."

"What do you mean?"

"He bored 'em out!" Annie shouts with delight. "You was always talkin' about doin' that, Kyle. I never thought you really would."

Kyle shrugs and looks at me. "A guy at a machine shop in Tampa owed me a favor," he explains. "These big block engines got enough steel around 'em, you can bore out the cylinders. Make 'em bigger."

"But wouldn't you need bigger pistons, too?"

"You can order those. Anyway, by the time you're all done, you don't got a 454 anymore. You got closer to 500 cubic inches total."

I stare at him in silence for a moment. Then, I shout

"WHOO-HOO!" and stick my head out the window. Up ahead, I can see the onramp to Interstate 65, our road to Chicago. With the damp nighttime air rushing into my face, I shout "TAKE THAT BAMA-LAMA! KYLE IS KING!"

Unfortunately, that's exactly when I spot the red flashing lights sweep across the Bel Air's chassis.

THIRTEEN

"Oh, man," Kyle says, pulling the Bel Air to the side of the road.

"What do they want?" Annie asks, her voice panicky. "You think our aunt and uncle already called the police?"

My head is still so focused on the race that the thought hadn't occurred to me. As soon as Annie says it, though, my heart starts doing a steeplechase, and I grasp for other explanations.

"Kyle, how fast were you going?"

He turns off the motor. "Not that fast."

"Is your license plate up-to-date?"

"Far as I know."

Leaving his headlights on, the sheriff's deputy—at least that's what I think he is—gets out of his car, and shining his flashlight beam, slowly approaches the driver's side window.

"Let me do the talkin'," Kyle tells us.

"How y'all doin?" the deputy greets us, but in a tone that says *I've got you now.*

"You in a big hurry tonight?" he continues.

"No, sir," Kyle says.

"That's not what I hear. I hear reports that someone with an old Bel Air was drag racin' out at Blackwell Bottoms."

So that's what this is about, I think.

I look at Annie and can see relief flow across her face.

Kyle keeps his voice in neutral. "I wouldn't know anything about that, Deputy."

The deputy sweeps his flashlight all along the Bel Air, and then into the back seat.

"How old are you, Miss?"

Annie doesn't hesitate. "Sixteen, sir."

Next, he shines the beam on me. "And you?"

"The same…sir."

"License and registration," the deputy tells Kyle.

Kyle gets them out and hands them to the man. After a moment, the deputy returns them.

Then, to our surprise, he drops his official tone of voice. "Let me tell y'all somethin'. Here in Blount County, we don't mind a little hot-roddin'. What we do mind is someone takin' advantage."

Kyle stares straight ahead as the deputy continues.

"Now, I don' know what you got under that hood, and I don' rightly care. But I'm afraid I am goin' to have to fine you for speedin' and reckless drivin' back there."

I expect Kyle to argue, but he simply asks, "How much?"

"Four hundred dollars."

"We don't have that much!" I blurt out.

The deputy glances at me. "A fine's a fine, son. Course if y'all would like to follow me down to the courthouse, we can discuss some other arrangements."

Kyle lets out a sigh and reaches into his shirt pocket. He counts out all his winnings—plus the eighty dollars he didn't bet.

"All I got is $380."

The deputy looks at me. "You got the extra $20?"

I shake my head. "That's everything."

The stricken look on my face must convince him. He takes the money from Kyle, stares at it, and says, "Well, let's just say you owe us. Next time through, you can give us the rest."

"Deputy, sir," Kyle asks. "I don't suppose you could see your way clear to let us keep twenty bucks to get home? We're almost out of gas."

The deputy silently regards Kyle. Then, he peels off a bill. "Here's five to make sure you get out of the county. Have a good night."

We stay parked by the side of the road as the deputy's cruiser pulls out and away.

"That deputy was probably friends with the drag racers," Annie complains. "He knew exactly how much money we had!"

"Now what?" I ask—to myself as much as anyone else. "Five bucks isn't going to get us anywhere."

Kyle pulls out his pack of cigarettes and lights one up. Staring straight ahead, he says, "Money ain't our only problem. If our aunt and uncle report us, it ain't gonna take three shakes for the sheriffs to put two 'n two together."

"Crap. You're right."

"What are we gonna do?" Annie's voice flutters with a renewed hint of panic.

"Well," Kyle says, "we got pulled over headin' north. Our aunt and uncle know we got people in Chicago."

"So we have to go somewhere else," Annie says.

Kyle looks at me. "Mike, you still up for goin' to Denver? Findin' that 1964 silver dollar and make us a million bucks?"

I chuckle half-heartedly. "Well, I don't know about finding the Peace dollar, but Denver sounds like a good destination—*if* we can get there."

Kyle exhales a cloud of smoke. "Yeah. Let's think on this a sec."

We sit there, minds churning while Kyle finishes his cigarette, but neither of us comes up with any brilliant ideas for raising cash.

Then, from the back seat, Annie's hand appears between us. In her palm sits a small wad of bills.

Kyle and I both spin around to gawk at her.

"You got money?" her brother asks.

"Where'd you get it?" I say.

Annie shrugs and gives us a half-smile. "I had about ten dollars saved up, but then I made some side bets on your race with that first Chevelle."

Kyle bursts out laughing. "How much did you win?" He takes the bills and begins counting.

"Reckon about thirty-five bucks," Annie tells him.

Kyle frowns. "That still won't get us there, not if we're gonna eat and have someplace to stay."

"Why can't we sleep in the car?" Annie asks.

Kyle stubs out his cigarette. "I guess we can."

"Well," I say. "Whatever we do, we'd better get moving."

FOURTEEN

Despite being pulled over next to the northbound onramp, Kyle and I decide to hightail it up Interstate 65.

"I want to get outta Alabama fast as possible," Kyle says, his fingers tight on the steering wheel. After stopping to use a few of our precious dollars to fill up with gas, he points the Bel Air straight north. Annie soon falls asleep in the back seat, but after the excitement of the last twelve hours, my synapses aren't about to settle down. Besides, I want to keep Kyle company on the drive.

He and I spend the first hour and a half recounting the previous day's events, and talking over what we should do next. Kyle keeps the Bel Air safely under the speed limit, and once or twice, we pass State Patrolmen, cruising or parked alongside the road. None of them give us any trouble, however, and finally, we cross the Alabama state line.

As we pass the sign that says "WELCOME TO TENNESSEE", both of us let out sighs of relief.

"Made it," Kyle says.

"Yeah. You think Alabama law enforcement would contact other states?"

"Do you?"

I shrug. "I don't know. I guess it all depends on how much fuss your aunt and uncle raise. What do you think they'll do?"

Kyle scratches his cheek. "I been thinkin' on that. If I was them, I'd wait 'til mornin' and then call the local police. I figure we got a day or two before things really heat up—*if* they decide to pursue it at all."

"Right now, they might just be worried about Annie," I say. "You going to let them know she's alright?"

Kyle again sighs. "I suppose I should call 'em—not that they deserve it with what my uncle's been doin'. Maybe later. Right now, I'm worried about how we're gonna get more cash."

"It's too bad we don't have one of our double eagles with us," I tell him. "Even a pawn shop would give us a few thousand for it."

"Believe me, I thought about that," Kyle says. "I just don't got no one I trust in Tampa to send me the thing. Not to mention that little detail of where we'd pick it up."

"Same here," I say. "If I called my mom and told her about it, she'd be all over me, wanting to know where I was, how I got the double eagle, why I needed her to send it, and on and on."

"We don't need that."

"Nope."

A minute passes and I yawn.

"You should rest up," Kyle tells me.

"I'm okay."

"I might need you to drive some later."

I look at him. "Really?" It hadn't occurred to me he'd actually let me drive the Bel Air.

"Sure. Or don't ya want to?"

He glances at me, and even by the dim glow of the dashboard, I see the glint in his eye.

I suppress a grin. "Okay. I'll rest."

I jam my sweatshirt against the door for a pillow and close my eyes. Within seconds, the rumble of the Bel Air's V-8 carries me into dreamland.

My eyes flicker open as Kyle drives us through the bright lights of Nashville, but I quickly drift off again. By the time I wake up for real, Kyle is pulling up alongside a curb, and I see the pale blue skin of morning stretched above us.

"Are we still in Tennessee?" I ask, sitting up and rolling my head around to stretch my neck.

Kyle harrumps as he kills the engine. "Tennessee? Boy, you slept through two states. We're in Missouri."

"Missouri?" Annie asks, her head popping up from the back seat.

I'm as surprised as she is. "What other state did we go through?"

"Cut through the corner of Kentucky before crossing into the Show Me State."

"What town is this?"

"Poplar Bluff. C'mon. I'm starvin'."

The three of us stiffly climb out of the Bel Air into the middle of an older downtown. Bricks pave the streets, and next to us stands a one-story wood-and-brick restaurant called Myrtle's Place. It looks strangely out-of-place next to the taller apartment and office buildings around it. However, there's no arguing with the sign that says "Breakfast Anytime".

After we hit the restrooms, a waitress seats us in an orange vinyl booth and gives us menus. A mix of truckers and businessmen surround us, slurping coffee, eating breakfast, and smoking cigarettes. We get a few stares, probably because of Kyle's and my whiskers and shaggy hair, but nobody bothers us.

After we order, I ask, "So what part of the state are we in?"

"Am guessing the southeast corner, but I don't rightly know," Kyle murmurs, keeping his voice low. "I just figured that after getting pulled over by that sheriff's deputy, we'd better get off the Interstate so I followed signs for Missouri. We could use some maps, but I hate spendin' money for 'em."

I glance over at a clock behind the lunch counter and see the hands just hitting seven. "This town look very big to you?"

"Big enough, I guess."

"Okay. I have an Automobile Club card. If there's an office here, I can get us all the maps we need."

Kyle raises an eyebrow. "What you doin' with an Auto Club card? You ain't even got your regular license, do you?"

"Just my learner's permit," I admit. "But my mom, she puts me on her family membership, just in case I get abducted by the SLA and my kidnappers get a flat tire."

"What's the SLA?" Annie asks.

"The Symbionese Liberation Army," I answer. "You know, the people who kidnapped Patty Hearst, the newspaper heiress?"

Annie gives me a blank look.

"It doesn't matter."

"Okay," Kyle continues. "Well at least we got the map problem figured. Now what about dough?"

I place my butter knife on my placemat and spin it slowly like a propeller. "I've been thinking about that," I say. "I might have an idea how we can raise a little cash."

"How?" Annie asks.

Before I can explain, the waitress brings us our meals. We inhale them, as my dad would say, and then sit and nurse our juice and coffee as the clock ticks toward 8:00.

"So," Kyle begins again. "You said you had an idea about raising some cash?"

I nod. "How much money do we have?"

Annie has decided that since most of our stash belonged to her, she should be the trip accountant. She looks at our breakfast bill, counts up our money, and says, "Breakfast is $7.30—"

"With a tip?" I ask.

She makes a face at me. "Call it $8.00. Subtract what we paid for gas last night, and we'll have $27.00 left."

"Yeah, but we need to fill up again, don't we?"

Kyle nods. "Soon."

"So that'll take us down to, what, $22.00?"

"Yep," Annie says.

"Shoot," I say. "That's barely enough to get started."

"What is this idea, anyway?" Kyle asks again.

I briefly explain to them what I have in mind.

"But," I say, "to get started, we're going to need a little more money. Either of you have anything you can pawn?"

Annie shakes her head. Kyle says, "I got some jumper cables, but we wouldn't get more than a buck or two for 'em. I also got some tools, but we'll probably need 'em. The Bel Air goes out of tune pretty fast."

We sit silently for another minute, then my face brightens. "Hey, wait a minute!"

I reach into my pocket and pull out the unused Greyhound bus ticket from Birmingham. "You think they'll let me cash this in?"

Kyle grins. "Worth a try."

FIFTEEN

When we pay the bill, I ask the cashier if there's a Triple-A office in town.

"No Auto Club," she answers. "You'll have to go someplace bigger for that. Which way you headed, Hon?"

I'm about to answer—who wouldn't after being called "Hon"? Fortunately, Kyle cuts in before me. "We're goin' to Memphis, ma'am."

"Oh," she says. "Well, they're sure to have an office there."

"What about a Greyhound bus station?" I ask. "Is there one here?"

She looks at me curiously—perhaps wondering why we need a bus station *and* road maps—but gives us the directions.

"Thank you, ma'am," Kyle says.

As we're climbing back into the Bel Air, I tell Kyle, "Thanks for catching me in there. I almost told her where we were going."

"We gotta be extra careful now," he cautions both me and Annie.

Even though we struck out with the Auto Club office, we get lucky at the Greyhound station. The clerk refunds my ticket, no questions asked. Even better, we find a huge road map mounted to the wall.

"Which way should we go?" Kyle asks, studying the map. "60 West toward Springfield?"

"Maybe for a while," I say. "But for what I've got in mind, we might want to get on even smaller roads. Maybe turn off here," I say, pointing to a gray line leading north off of 60.

As we walk back to the car, Kyle tells me, "I'm draggin', Mike. Can you take the wheel?"

"Sure, but it's almost 9:00. Let's hit a bank first."

"To try out this scheme of yours? You really think it's gonna work?"

"Maybe. I don't know."

"Oooo-kay."

Kyle drives back downtown, to a large stone building on Main with a cool-looking clock raised above the street, and the words "Bank of Poplar Bluff" carved along the top.

"This what you need?" he asks.

I study it. "I think so."

"You want us to come in with you?" Annie asks.

"No. Not the first time."

I've told Annie and Kyle my plan for getting money, but am feeling less certain about it now. I also don't want to raise any suspicions by having Annie along. I get out of the car and glance around me. Quite a few people are out and about, walking the sidewalks, opening up stores, starting to shop.

I take a deep breath and walk into the bank, trying to look as confident as I can. The bank is a nice one and has a row of ornate, old-fashioned teller windows to one side of a large lobby. I pick out a younger-looking teller and walk up to her.

She smiles sweetly. "Good morning. May I help you?"

I pull out three ten-dollar bills—most of the money we have left—and ask, "Can I buy some rolls of half dollars, please?"

I expect a strange look, or a question why I need

them, but the teller just takes the money, and says, "Sure."

I watch as she opens a drawer full of coin rolls of every denomination, wrapped in paper. She grabs three short, stubby rolls with the words "HALVES—$10" on them and plonks them down with a thud.

"Th-thanks," I say.

"It's my pleasure. You need anything else today, sir?"

"No…ma'am."

"You have a nice day, now."

"You, too," I tell her, and scurry out of the bank.

"Did you get 'em?" Annie asks as I jump back into the Bel Air.

"Yep," I say, handing them each a roll.

"So what are we lookin' for?"

Kyle answers for me. "Pull out any half dollars dated 1970 or older. That right, Big Mike?"

"Yeah. We're hoping to get Kennedy halves dated between 1965 and 1969. If we're lucky, we might get something older."

"And we're doin' this because there's real silver in 'em?" Annie asks.

"That's right," I tell her, eagerly tearing open my roll.

I don't have any idea what I'll find. Even though I've been collecting coins for years, I mostly look for specific dates to plug into my coin albums. I've never looked through half dollar rolls at all, figuring I already had all the dates I could find. As soon as I peel away the paper wrapper, though, I feel my adrenaline pump.

"Eureka," I quietly say. Looking at the sides of the coins in my hands, I can tell that some of them are silver.

"You got somethin'?" Kyle asks.

"Yeah, but I'm not sure what yet."

"Hey, here's a 1968!" Annie shouts in back.

"I got one, too," Kyle says.

We quickly sort through all of our half dollars and when we're through, I'm amazed.

"I've got eight between 1965 and 1970," I say. "What about you?"

"Ten," Kyle answers.

"Eleven!" Annie says.

"Wow!" I say, with a grin. "Anyone find anything 1964 or older?"

"No," they both answer.

"That's okay. This is still a great haul."

"How much they worth?" Kyle asks.

"I haven't figured that out," I tell them. "Each of these half dollars we found is 40% silver, and I think the price of silver is about $4.50 an ounce. If you figure roughly that two half dollars together weigh an ounce, and multiply that by .4, you get—"

"$1.80 for two, or about .90 apiece," Annie says.

I look at Annie and then Kyle. He shrugs. "Annie's always been a whiz with numbers."

"So," Annie continues. "We got us twenty-nine half dollars. That should be worth about $26. We almost double our money!"

"Yeah," I say, "but I'm not sure each half dollar really weighs half an ounce. They might weigh less. And we still have to find someone—a coin dealer, probably—to buy these things."

"Still," Kyle says. "That ain't bad."

"Too bad we didn't get anything older than 1965."

"What's the difference with those?" Annie asks, suddenly *very* interested in coins.

"Well, before 1965, the half dollars—like the quarters and dimes—were made of 90% silver."

"So they were worth more than twice as much?"

"Yep."

"So what now?"

"Well, we put these 40% silver halves aside, turn in the rest for cash, and then hit another bank for some fresh rolls."

"Not me," Kyle moans. "I gotta sleep."

"That's okay, Brother," Annie tells him. "You sleep while Mike and me make us some money!"

SIXTEEN

O n our way out of town, Kyle stops at another bank so I can turn in our "clad", or non-silver, half dollars for regular cash. Adding in the extra money we had before the last bank, we barely scrape up enough to get two ten-dollar bills back from the cashier.

"This is goin' to be slow," Kyle observes, handing Annie the money.

"Yeah, but I don't know what other choice we have," I say.

"You guys don't know what you're talkin' about," Annie tells us. "We're gonna get rich!"

Kyle and I both laugh at her enthusiasm.

Kyle drives the Bel Air to a big, deserted parking lot at the edge of town, and he and I trade seats.

"You ever drive a clutch before?" he asks.

"My dad started teaching me last summer," I say, "but his truck has the gear shift on the steering column."

"This'll be easier. The gears are in a simple "H" pattern. Just press in the clutch, and turn the ignition."

I look over at him. "What if I crash?"

"You won't."

I take a deep breath, turn the key, and the Bel Air roars to life. The monster pistons send vibrations through the steering wheel and up my arms before rattling every vertebra in my backbone.

"Let's practice driving around the parking lot a couple of times," Kyle says. "Put her into first, ease out the clutch, and give her a little gas."

I follow his instructions—sort of.

Instead of easing out the clutch, I jerk my left foot up while barely tapping the gas pedal. The Bel Air lurches forward three times like a gasping whale, then dies.

"Good one," Annie says.

"Annie, be quiet," Kyle tells her.

She snickers, and my face glows.

"Sorry about that," I say.

"This time give it more gas."

I start the car again, and proceed to give it too much gas as I let out the clutch. The Bel Air jerks forward, but at least doesn't stall.

"Okay, good," Kyle tells me. "We're moving. Speed up and shift it into second gear."

"In this parking lot?" I say, my voice a little shriller than I'd prefer.

"Sure. There's no one else here. Just give her some more gas, put in the clutch, and pull the stick back into second."

I roll to the edge of the parking lot and coast through a U-turn, then speed up.

"Now!" Kyle tells me.

I push in the clutch, but forget to ease off the gas when I pull the stick shift back. The engine slams into second and the Bel Air bolts forward.

"Whoo-Hoo! This is better than bumper cars at the fair," Annie shouts.

Kyle turns to her. "Annie, will you close that crab trap 'a yours? Don't listen to her Mike, you're doin' great. Now just head out to the highway."

"*Already?* You said we were going to practice."

"We did. Now it's time to drive."

"Kyle, I—"

"Don't worry. You're gonna do fine."

"I don't—"

"Just wake me when we get to Denver."

"Yeah, right."

As I do another couple of laps around the parking lot, Kyle climbs over into the back seat, and Annie replaces him as my copilot. Reluctantly, I steer toward the highway and stop. I look both ways, and—

Kill the motor again.

"Kyle," I begin to protest, but he's already got his eyes closed.

Annie looks at me, a mischievous grin on her face. "Just you and me, now."

Even through my driving jitters, I pause an extra second to look at her, and I have to admit, I'm feeling a little smitten. Wisps of her blonde hair are sticking out, backlit by the morning sun, and her face seems even prettier than it did yesterday.

Stop it, Mike, I tell myself. *She's three years younger than you are!* But that doesn't seem to calm the sudden acceleration of my pulse.

With renewed concentration, I restart the Bel Air, check for traffic, and bolt out onto the highway.

"Denver, here we come!" Annie shouts.

Leaving Poplar Bluff, the road quickly begins twisting and turning through beautiful forested hills—what they call "mountains" around here. I get the Bel Air up to third gear and keep it there to avoid having to downshift, something I'm not quite sure how to do. We pass a sign that says "Mark Twain National Forest" and another reading "Gateway to the Ozarks." I try to relax at the wheel.

"We need some tunes," Annie says, turning on the radio. She fiddles with the dial, but only finds a couple of static-y Country stations. "Forget that," she says, and reaches under the seat.

"Ah-ha!"

"What?" I ask, not daring to look over.

"Tapes," she tells me. "What kinda music you like?"

"What do you have?"

"It's all Kyle's stuff. Allman Brothers. Marshall Tucker. New one by the Outlaws? You know 'em?"

"I don't think so. But—"

"Ah, now we're talkin'!" Before I can put in my request, she selects a different tape and shoves it into the eight-track tape player below the radio. She presses a button, and I hear the clunk as the player shifts tracks. A second later, some trumpets issue three sharp notes, and an infectious piano rhythm picks up, followed by the high falsetto voice of Eddie Kendricks singing "Booooogie. Boogie down Ba-by!"

Annie twists the volume knob clockwise.

"Shouldn't we keep it down?" I ask, motioning to Kyle.

"Ah, my brother'll sleep through a train wreck."

I'm not crazy about Annie's choice of metaphors, but I risk glancing back to see that indeed, Kyle is sprawled out like a tranquilized leopard.

"You like soul music?" Annie asks, already grooving in her seat.

"Well," I admit. "I'm more into hard rock, but I always kind of liked this song."

"The Temptations are the best," Annie says.

"Wait. I thought this was Eddie Kendricks."

Annie shoots me an amused look. "Mike, where you been, anyways? Kendricks was lead singer for the Temptations before headin' out on his own."

"Oh," I mutter, but let the steady bass line pound away my embarrassment.

"Have you ever been to the Ozarks before?" I ask Annie.

"I never been *anywhere.*"

"I've never been here, either. It's pretty."

I grip the steering wheel tighter as we drive through a steep bend in the road. Annie asks, "You live in California during the school year? What's California like—I mean, besides not having any good music?"

"Very funny," I say, seizing the gear shift as we go up a hill. I am thinking I might have to downshift, but to my relief the Bel Air powers up the grade no sweat. With that crisis past, I think about Annie's question.

"I don't know. California's nice."

"Are there palm trees there, like in Florida?"

"Yeah, but not out in the mountains. See all the different kinds of maples, pines, oaks, dogwoods, and other trees here? In California, you pretty much just see oak trees—oh, and eucalyptus trees from Australia."

"What about the beaches. Do you surf?"

I shake my head. "A lot of the 'loadies' do—you know, the guys who use drugs—but I'm too busy with school to do that. Surf, I mean."

"What are you busy with?"

"Homework, mostly. In the fall, I run cross-country, and in the spring, I run track."

"I'd like to go to California," Annie muses. "It's gotta

be better than Alabama."

I shrug. "I don't know. It's just different. I like Florida a lot."

"Is that why you're so anxious to get back there?"

I glance over at her and see the familiar glint in her eyes. I chuckle, but feel guilty, thinking about my dad. "I want to go back. Just not yet."

I pause for a few seconds, then say, "I'm sorry about… I mean, that things with your aunt and uncle…"

Annie waves her hand as if brushing it off, and turns to look out her window. "It's over now. I'm just glad I don't ever have to go back."

Don't be so sure of that, I think, but don't say anything.

We continue driving through national forest lands as Eddie Kendricks lapses into some slower ballads that I don't like as much. At a place called Winona, we turn north onto an even smaller road, but keep rolling. Now that I've got the Bel Air moving, I don't want to stop because I might never get it going again. Eventually, though, we come to a little town called Eminence, and I have no choice but to slow down.

"Shoot," I say, braking behind a pick-up truck. The truck is stopped in the middle of the road, talking to another truck stopped in the opposite direction. I glance back at Kyle in the back seat, hoping he's ready to drive again, but he's still out cold.

Annie laughs. "Don't be so serious," she says. "You look like you're ridin' on top of a wild tiger."

"I am!"

"No, you ain't. Just remember, your gas foot and your clutch foot go in opposite directions."

"How would *you* know?"

"You think Kyle didn't teach me how to drive?"

"*You can drive?*"

"With a motor head for a brother? 'Course I can drive!"

"Well, why aren't *you* driving instead of *me*?"

Annie shrugs. "Ain't got no license."

"Neither do I!"

"You got your learner's permit, ain't you? 'Sides, Kyle wanted you to."

Just then, the pickup truck moves. Despite Annie's advice, I again pop the clutch and the Bel Air lurches forward, almost stalling.

"Look," Annie tells me. "There's a bank up ahead. Let's stop and get some more half dollars."

Do we have to? I think, but steer the Bel Air to the side of the street and park.

SEVENTEEN

I let Annie go into the bank this time and she emerges with two fresh half dollar rolls. She slides back into the passenger seat and gives me a roll.

I tear it open and quickly flip through the half dollars. "Shoot. Nothing. What about you?"

"Me, neither. But what's this?" Annie says, handing me a metal disc a little smaller than a half dollar.

"Where did you find this?" I ask.

"In the half dollar roll."

"Well, it's not a half dollar," I tell her.

"Duh."

I angle the object so that I can read it better, and see that it has a picture of a dove on one side and a peace sign on the other. Under the dove, along the rim, are the words "Love Dollar" and above it, "Stop the War". On the other side, it reads, "Redeemable for Peace, Freedom, and Understanding".

"Huh."

"You ever seen one 'a those before?" Annie asks.

"No. Have you?"

She laughs. "Not hardly. Is it worth anything?"

"I doubt it. Looks like we just got robbed of fifty cents."

"And no silver, neither."

"Maybe someone around here is searching for silver halves, too," I tell her, slipping the "Love Dollar" into my pocket. "We'll just have to try somewhere else."

From Eminence, the countryside just gets prettier

and prettier. The road continues winding through a mix of hardwood and pine forest, and up and around hills and ridgelines. We cross two narrow stone bridges, over a pair of clear rivers.

"Ozark National Scenic Riverways," Annie reads as we pass a sign. "Look, there's some people canoeing."

Twenty miles later, in Salem, we again stop to exchange our clad halves for bills. Annie replaces Eddie Kendricks with the Allman Brothers, which I like better, but Kyle keeps sawing logs.

"Man, he must really be wiped," I say, as I pull back out onto the road.

"I'm surprised he drove long as he did," Annie says.

"You want to drive?"

"Not me. If we get stopped, I'm in enough trouble."

"Thanks a lot."

At Rolla, we try another bank, and this time do better than in Eminence. A lot better. Between Annie and me, we find twenty-one 40% silver half dollars and one 1964 90% silver half.

"That's what I'm talking about," I tell Annie. "We should probably find a place to sell them."

"What about lunch?"

"That'll cost money. The more money we can use to buy halves, the faster we'll be able to build up some cash."

"I don't care. I want food."

I could also eat, but don't want to admit it to Annie. By now, though, I am finally getting the hang of the clutch and gear shift, and I stop at a convenience store outside of Jefferson City so Annie can buy some snacks.

As she opens her door to get out, I say, "Ask if there's a Triple-A office around here. And don't spend too much."

"I'm buyin' the whole store," she shoots back, slamming the door.

My eyes follow the back pockets of her jeans as she walks into the store, and I again try to squash the romantic feelings working through me. While she's shopping, I also consider whether I should give my dad a call, but then remember that I just talked to him sixteen hours ago. With all that's happened in the past two days, it seems like I've been gone a month.

Still, I should call him tomorrow to let him know I'm okay.

I glance back at Kyle and confirm that he's still sleeping and, not for the first time, I worry about what he and Annie are getting themselves into. The word *fugitives* pops into my mind, and I wonder what their aunt and uncle are going to do—and what that might mean for my friends. I know that Kyle wouldn't have taken Annie if it wasn't serious, but Annie seems strangely disconnected to their situation, and to how her uncle was treating her back in Alabama.

She's probably just hiding it well, I think.

On cue, Annie comes back to the car, carrying a paper sack full of groceries.

"What'd you get?" I ask, my stomach rumbling.

"Nothing for you," she teases.

"Hey! Hand it over."

"You said you weren't hungry."

I lunge at her and wrestle for the bag. She squeals and fights me off, laughing. She's wiry and strong—stronger than she looks—and grappling with her, I feel my pulse again quicken—and not because I want food.

Finally, she relents and hits me in the chest with a bag of Fritos. "Don't hog them," she warns.

I settle back behind the steering wheel, and let my pulse downshift. After shoving a handful of chips into my mouth, I ask, "Did you get the directions to the AAA?"

She unwraps a pair of Twinkies. "Keep drivin' into town and turn on Missouri Boulevard."

I start up the Bel Air and pull back out onto the highway. We pass Lincoln University, and I catch glimpses of the Missouri River and the state capitol building to our right.

"This looks like a cool town," I say.

"There's Missouri Boulevard up there."

We find the AAA office, and Annie and I go in together. We're served by a woman with a hairdo that's taller than the capitol dome nearby. She wears oversized glasses and regards us suspiciously when I ask for the maps. I can tell she doesn't want to give them to me, but when I flash her my AAA card, she reluctantly slaps them down.

Before leaving, I ask her, "Do you know where there are any coin shops around here?"

"No," she says, impatiently, "but here's a phone book. You can try the Yellow Pages."

"Do you have a pen and paper?" I ask.

She gives an audible huff and hands them over. Annie and I take them to a nearby table.

"What a hag," Annie whispers to me as we sit down. "Thinks she's so much better 'n us."

I don't answer, but flip through the Yellow Pages until I find the heading "Coins".

Three stores are listed, including a couple of pawnshops, and I write down an address that I think we already passed.

I nudge Annie. "C'mon, let's go."

Coin shops are pretty much the same wherever you go, and when we walk into Jefferson City Stamp and Coin, I feel like I've been there a hundred times before. The moment Annie and I open the door, a loud electronic "pong" alerts the shopkeeper that he's got customers, and a musty smell of mildew and cigarette smoke fills our noses. In front of us, waist-high glass cabinets with trays of coins and stamps fill the floor of the shop like a giant horseshoe. Many of the glass cases have black buttons that let you rotate the trays of coins back and forth like little Ferris wheels to find what you're looking for.

"Help you?" asks a man sitting in a green vinyl chair at a desk. He's holding a magnifying glass, and coins are spread in front of him. Over to the side is a little black-and-white television set with the volume turned low.

Annie hands me the two-and-a-half rolls of 40% silver half dollars we've scraped together, and I set them down on a glass display case. "Do you buy 40% Kennedy halves?"

"How many ya got?" the man asks, still not getting up from his chair.

"Fifty-two."

"Fifty-two rolls?"

"No, uh, halves."

"Nah. More trouble 'n their worth. If you had a thousand, five hunnert, maybe we could talk."

"Oh."

I stand there for a moment, then ask, "You know anyone who does buy them around here?"

The guy spreads his hand over his mouth and slowly rubs his jaw. "Nah."

"Okay, thanks," I mumble, thinking, *Thanks for nothing.*

As we walk toward the door, though, the guy surprises me. "Hey," he calls after us. "Try Downtown Coins over in Warrensburg. I hear they sometimes do a business in halves. Tell 'em Bob in Jeff City sent you."

Annie whispers to me, "I'll tell 'em Bob can't get up offa his lazy butt!"

EIGHTEEN

When we exit the shop, we're surprised to find Kyle leaning against the Bel Air, munching on a handful of Fritos.

"You're alive!" I exclaim.

Kyle rubs an eye socket with his free hand. "Kinda. Where are we?"

"Jefferson City," Annie answers, "and ready to get outta here!"

"Why? What's goin' on?"

I briefly recount our experiences with the AAA lady and Mr. Coin Shop Owner. Kyle's more concerned with the outcomes than with the rude manners we've run into.

"So we got the maps, but no dough?"

"Yeah, but maybe we'll have some luck in Warrensburg—wherever that is."

I reach into the Bel Air and pull out our new stack of maps. I unfold the Missouri state map, Annie looking over my shoulder.

"There's Warrensburg," she points. "It's in the direction we're headin'."

I scan the map in my hands. "What's the scale on this thing?" I ask, more to myself than to her or Kyle. After locating it, I measure the distance with my fingers. "Looks like Warrensburg's about a hundred miles from here. Now that we're out of the Ozarks, ought to be a straight shot."

"What time is it?" Kyle asks.

"Little after two," Annie says.

"We ought to be able to make it before that coin store

closes," I say.

Kyle pops the final Fritos into his mouth. "Let's go."

We climb back into the Bel Air, Kyle again at the wheel. "Man, I needed that sleep," he says. "Thanks for drivin'."

I shrug and try to act cool. "Piece of cake."

"He only stalled it six times," Annie says, "and he almost ran over four pedestrians—including an old blind lady!"

I give her a sour face. "Very funny."

"See? I knew you could do it," Kyle tells me. Then, to Annie, he says, "If you don't be quiet, I'm gonna make you drive."

Annie cackles and settles back in her seat, but I have to admit I am relieved Kyle is back at the helm.

He keeps the Bel Air under the speed limit, but even so, the drive to Warrensburg passes quickly. We cruise along U.S. 50, a more-or-less straight road running through hilly farm country mixed with patches of deciduous trees. We stop along the way at a bank in Sedalia and score another five 40% half dollars before rolling into our destination.

Warrensburg isn't nearly as big as Jefferson City, but has a friendlier feel to it. We turn left on what looks like a major street, and soon pass a cluster of attractive limestone buildings and a large sign reading "Central Missouri State University". On the left, I see long brick buildings that look like dormitories.

"Not many students around," Kyle observes.

"Probably out for summer," I tell him. "My dad's university looks the same way right now."

"Where do you think this coin shop is?"

I see a couple of girls wearing mini skirts walking along the sidewalk.

"Pull over," I tell Kyle.

"We're trying to find the shop, not pick up women," Annie tells me.

"Ha. Ha," I say, and lean out the window.

The girls turn at the rumble of the Bel Air's engine.

"Excuse me," I say. "Do you happen to know where there's a coin shop around here?"

The girls look at each other, not sure what to make of us, but the closest one—a pretty brunette—flashes me a smile. "I think maybe there's one downtown, near the furniture store."

"Downtown?"

"Oh, turn around and go past the train tracks and hang a left. Go down until you hit Holden. That's the main street. Jog to the right, and I think you'll see it."

"Thanks."

"Nice car," she tells Kyle as we pull away.

Annie hits Kyle on the shoulder. "That girl *wants* you, Brother. You should offer her a ride."

"Annie, will you quit being such a pest?" Kyle says, but when we pull a U-turn, he honks to the two girls and guns past them.

Kyle turns left on Railroad Street and we roll down a hill to a small downtown area. The downtown actually looks a lot livelier than a lot of the places we've passed through, probably because of the college nearby. We find the street the pretty brunette told us about and spot Downtown Coins just past a family-owned furniture store.

All three of us go into the coin shop, and see the owner talking to another customer.

"Be right with you," he tells us.

"Well, at least this guy has some manners," Annie murmurs.

Annie and Kyle start playing with the black buttons that move the coins around in the display cases, but I notice a stack of *Coin Universe* newspapers on a counter. On top is the same issue I have in my AWOL bag, and I again am drawn to the article about the 1964 Peace dollar.

"That's quite a story, isn't it?" the dealer asks, walking over to me after finishing with his other customer.

Surprised, I look up. "Oh. Yeah, it is. Do you think any of these Peace dollars survived the melting?"

"I don't know," the owner says, as Kyle and Annie wander over to listen. "But I know at least one dealer that was advertising for them."

"Whaddya mean?" Kyle asks.

The man looks thoughtful, then says, "Hang on a second."

He walks through a curtain into a back room and reappears a minute later, carrying an older copy of *Numismatics Weekly*. He flips to the back and says, "Ah!"

He punches his finger down on an ad in the classified section. It's from a coin dealer in New Jersey:

> *** **REWARD** ***
> $3,000 DOLLARS paid for 1964-D Peace
> Dollar, no questions asked. Will take as many
> as offered.

"Three thousands dollars!" Annie exclaims.

The dealer scoffs. "Oh, this guy was low-balling. If any of these coins exist, they're worth six figures if they're worth a dime."

Annie quickly does the calculation while Kyle and I raise eyebrows at each other.

"You mean $100,000?" Annie asks.

The dealer shrugs. "Maybe a lot more. Only problem is, the coins might not be legal."

"How's that?" I ask.

"Well, this ad came out in 1973, two years ago. Apparently, it got government officials worried that some of the 1964 dollars really had slipped through their fingers. The U.S. Mint released a threatening notice that any 1964 Peace dollars that turned up would be confiscated. Right after that, this dealer quit running ads to buy them."

"So you're sayin'…" Kyle asks.

The man drums his fingers on the glass counter in front of him. "Well, it's kind of a good news-bad news thing, isn't it? The fact that the Mint threatened collectors about the coin tells me that there's an excellent chance some of these Peace dollars survived getting melted. On the other hand, with the Mint's nasty press release, the chances of any of the coins surfacing is close to zero."

"So you're saying they're pretty much worthless?"

The dealer raises his hands, "Oh, I didn't say *that*! In fact, I'd bet good money that quite a few coin collectors are actively looking for these coins, and that if they do exist, more than one wealthy person has paid good money for them. Just don't expect to see them on display at any coin shows or museums."

Kyle, Annie, and I all look at each other.

"So," the owner says, "what can I do for you today?"

NINETEEN

We exit the coin shop with forty dollars in our pockets—or Annie's pockets, to be more precise. By now, all of us are tired of being cooped up in the car all day, so we decide to go for a stroll to stretch our legs. Annie walks between Kyle and me.

"Wow," I tell them both. "We didn't make as much from those halves as I thought we would. Sorry about that. I thought they were worth more than they really are."

Kyle shrugs. "We made ten bucks profit. That ain't bad."

"Enough for two tanks of gas," Annie confirms.

"Besides, forget the half dollars," Kyle continues. "What I'm thinkin' about is those Peace dollars."

"Yeah," Annie chimes in, as we walk down to Holden and turn right, back toward the university.

I look at both of them, surprised. "You didn't seem that excited when I told you about them before."

"No offense, Mike, but you didn't make 'em seem real before. After what that coin guy told us, it sounds like those Peace dollars are out there, sure as the sidewalk we're walkin' on."

"Okay," I say, "but even if they are, you heard the guy. Who's going to admit it? If one of these coins shows up anywhere, the Mint's going to swoop in and seize it."

Kyle pauses to look for traffic as we cross the street. "Mike, if these coins are worth as much as we think, there are ways to move 'em, believe me!"

Now, I am the one feeling skeptical. "So what are

you thinking? We just roll into Denver and start asking around?"

"Why not? The Mint is still there, and it's only been ten years. Some of the guys who helped make the Peace dollars still got to be working there, right?"

"I suppose."

"Sure!" Annie joins in. "We just wait until they get off work and ask 'em some questions."

I shake my head. "I don't know."

"What're you talkin' about?" Kyle asks. "This was your idea to begin with."

We reach the university campus and follow a concrete walkway diagonally across it. The sun is low, and the heat is giving the first signs of releasing its grip on the day. Birds and squirrels are moving around in trees, and the handsome limestone and brick buildings cast welcome shadows across our path.

"It just seemed like a better idea before," I tell them. "If there are—were—any 1964 Peace dollars, they're probably all locked away in the safes of big money collectors by now."

"Not if some Mint employees got 'em and are too scared to try to get rid of 'em."

"But Kyle," I say. "They're not just going to *give* them to us. They're going to want to be paid. How are we going to do that?"

Kyle scratches the blond stubble on his cheek. "I ain't got that part worked out yet, but we'll come up with somethin'. I'm just sayin', if those Peace dollars are still there, who better to find them than us?"

I again think about finding the Confederate double eagles two years ago. It took Kyle and me weeks to figure out where they were hidden, but we didn't give up.

If we really put our minds to this Peace dollar thing..., I start to think, but then I reject the notion.

"The double eagles were different," I say out loud.

Annie's head snaps toward me. "What double eagles? What *are* double eagles?"

"Oops," I say.

We all halt next to a stone chapel in the center of campus. Kyle tries to explain. "Me and Mike found us some gold coins back at Shipwreck Island a couple of years ago."

Annie looks first at me, then at Kyle. Then, she shoves her brother with both hands. "You never told me that! You still got 'em? Can we sell 'em?"

Already, I am wishing I could take back any mention of the double eagles.

"No," Kyle tells Annie. "We don't have 'em with us, and besides, that ain't the point. The point is that if we all work together, I'm sayin' we can track down these silver dollars, too. Whaddya say, Mike. You in?"

"I'm in!" Annie confirms.

I stare from one to the other of them. Finally, I say, "I'm not saying I am or I'm not. I'll decide when we get to Denver—and first, we have to get there."

Kyle and Annie flash me nearly identical grins.

"Fair enough," Kyle says.

"A bigger question," I tell them, "is what we're going to do tonight. Do you want to drive all night again?"

"I could if I had to," Kyle says, "but I'd like to get me a good night's sleep."

"I want a real bathroom," Annie complains.

"Even a cheap motel room's going to cost ten bucks,"

I say. "If we're going to keep doing the half dollar thing, that's going to eat into our seed money."

"I'm hungry," Annie says.

"Me, too," I tell her, "but I think we have to choose. Food or motel."

As we start walking back toward our car, I raise another difficult subject. Near the university student union, I spot a row of pay phones and point to them.

"You going to call your aunt and uncle?"

Kyle's whole body tenses. "I guess I should."

"Why?" Annie exclaims. "What we're doin' is none 'a their business!"

Kyle turns to her. "C'mon, Annie. I just want 'em to know you're safe. They got a right to that."

Panic floods Annie's face. "But they'll find out where we are!"

"They won't," Kyle tells her. "I'll just make it quick and not tell 'em anything besides we're okay."

"Kyle, I don't want to go back there!"

"You won't, but I'm callin' 'em," Kyle says, anger creeping into his voice. "Mike, you got any change?"

I find half a dozen quarters in my pockets, and hand them to him. Annie stomps away to sulk, but I walk with Kyle to the pay phones.

"You want me to leave?" I ask.

"Naw. To tell the truth, I appreciate you bein' here. This ain't a call I'm lookin' forward to."

Kyle dials '0', and even though I'm standing a few feet away, I can clearly hear the various operators as Kyle gives them the phone number and is told how much the call will cost.

Kyle puts in the coins and his jaw tenses as the phone

starts ringing on the other end.

A woman's voice answers—his aunt, I'm guessing.

Kyle clears his throat. "It's me, Kyle."

"*Kyle!* Thank god! What in heavens is goin' on! Where are you? Have you got Annie?"

"She's with me, and we're both fine."

With that news, the voice on the other end hardens. "Why didn't you tell us you were coming? Just what in Hades do you think y'all are doin?"

"Annie don't wanna live with you anymore."

"We couldn't care less what she *wants*! We're her legal guardians, and you'd better return her right this minute. The police are already lookin' for you."

"I'm not bringin' her back," Kyle says, his voice growing louder.

"If you bring her back now, we won't press charges," his aunt warns.

"She ain't comin' back."

"Kyle, you and me, we got our differences, but you can't even dream how much trouble you're about to land in."

"You let me worry about that. Annie's not safe with you. She knows it and I know it, and if you try to have the police find me, I'll tell 'em everything I know."

Her aunt pauses, and in a more subdued voice asks, "What are you talkin' about, Kyle? Whadda you mean Annie's not safe?"

"You know what I'm talkin' about."

"No," the aunt says coldly. "I don't."

Her denial only makes Kyle madder. "Have it your way!"

TWENTY

Kyle slams down the receiver and savagely searches for his pack of smokes. His hands shake trying to light the match, but he gets a cigarette going and inhales deeply.

He curses and mutters, "Why'd all this have to happen?"

"I don't know," I answer lamely.

"I knew they were gonna react that way. They probably got the whole state of Alabama lookin' for us, and all I'm tryin' to do is protect my sister from that son-of-a..."

His voice trails off.

"I know," I tell him.

Then, for want of something better to say, I ask, "What's your uncle like, anyway? Has he always been violent?"

"I don't know, but he's one of these Holy Roller types, know what I mean?"

"Not exactly."

Kyle waves his hand so that his cigarette tip cuts an orange streak through the air. "When we was growin' up, he was a regular guy. He worked for a local bottle distributor—Coke or Pepsi or somethin'. He drank and smoked and was a good 'ole boy. He even took me and Annie fishin'."

"What happened?"

"I don' know exactly, but suddenly he went and got religion."

"You mean like a Born-Again Christian?"

"Oh, that don't begin to describe it, Mike. Suddenly, everything was God This, and God That, and nobody was actin' good and righteous enough for him. Even became some kinda minister at some lil church where he could rail on about sinners 'n hell 'n hippies 'n commies. I don' know how my aunt has stood it all these years. That's a big reason I fought to get Annie to stay with me after Momma died. Annie and me didn't grow up like that. I knew it'd crush her."

Kyle takes another hurricane-force drag on the cigarette and stares at me. "And then I get Annie's letter about him hittin' her. What a hypocrite!"

Kyle flings his cigarette to the ground and starts walking back toward Annie.

I step on the burning butt and catch up to him.

"I mean, what else could I do?" Kyle asks me.

"I don't know. I think maybe you did the right thing— if you can get away with it. It's just not going to be easy."

"You're tellin' me."

"Look," I say. "Maybe your aunt was trying to scare you. Maybe she won't get the authorities after you."

"She will."

"Well, then, we just have to be smarter than them until things cool down and they quit looking for you."

We reach the stone bench where Annie's sitting, but keep talking.

"They still don't know where you are," I say. "That's a big advantage. Another is that you can get work anywhere, can't you?"

Kyle nods. "Yeah. Cars always break down and need fixin'. What about Canada, Mike? You think we should go there?"

"I don't want to go to Canada," Annie says.

Kyle ignores her. "All them draft dodgers are up there. I figure I get in touch with some of 'em, they can set us up."

"Didn't President Ford pardon them?" I ask. "Have they started coming back to the States already?"

"I don' know, Mike. It was just an idea."

Neither of us says anything for a few moments. Then Annie stands up. "Well, wherever we're goin', I'm still hungry and I still want a shower."

Kyle glares at her and she glares back at him. Then, suddenly, the ice breaks and they both laugh.

I join in. "She's got a point."

"Yeah," Kyle admits. "I know. I been thinkin' about that, too. Mike, weren't those dormitories we saw on the other side of campus?"

"I think so."

"And the students are probably gone for the summer?"

"Yeah…"

Kyle motions us with his hand. "C'mon. Let's go."

We head back to the street where the coin shop and the Bel Air are, and decide to spend ten of our precious dollars on a good dinner at a place called Heroes Restaurant. We actually could have eaten two meals apiece, but knew we'd need the rest of our cash to keep swappin' out half dollars, looking for silver.

After dinner, we drive over to the university dormitories. Kyle steers through a vast, empty parking lot and parks the Bel Air so that it's hidden back behind one of the buildings.

"Wait here," Kyle tells us, and disappears for a while.

When he returns, he says, "Get your bags."

Annie and I look at each other, curious, but grab our stuff and follow him into a dormitory through the back door, and then up to a pair of rooms. The rooms share a bathroom and have two twin beds each.

"This is for *us*?" I ask.

Kyle just grins.

"How'd you swing it?"

He shrugs. "Just told the custodian our situation—more or less."

"And it won't cost us anything?"

"Nope. There's even hot water, and he threw in some towels, sheets, and blankets," Kyle says, motioning to a stack of linens on the nearest bed.

I shake my head in wonder. "I think I'm beginning to like Warrensburg, Missouri."

Kyle laughs.

Annie grabs a towel and shouts, "I get the first shower."

That night, Annie takes one of the dorm rooms while Kyle and I share the other. Exhausted from the past two days, we all sleep in the next morning, but finally, I hear robins outside and Annie taking another shower in the bathroom. I roll over to see morning light streaming in through our windows.

"You awake?" Kyle asks.

I groan and look over at him. "Almost. You sleep okay?"

"For a while. Then I woke up thinkin' about my aunt and uncle, and what they might be doin'."

"Well, we'll find out soon enough, won't we? I figure it's fifty-fifty they'll drop it—especially after you basically said you know all about your uncle beating up on Annie."

"Maybe…" Kyle says, doubtfully.

"Anyway, the farther we get from Alabama, the better our chances are. As far as they know, we're in Chicago right now."

"You think they could trace my phone call?"

"I doubt it."

Just then, Annie bursts in, her wet hair hanging over her shoulders and her long, tanned legs sticking out of a pair of clean cut-off jeans. I notice she's wearing a T-shirt from the University of West Florida.

"Hey, that's mine!" I protest, sitting up. "I didn't say you could wear that."

She puts her hand on her hip and stares at me provocatively. "Didn't say I couldn't, neither."

Kyle laughs and shakes his head, "Women."

I scowl at Annie, thinking, *That T-shirt's having more luck with women than I've ever had.*

TWENTY-ONE

We do an especially thorough job cleaning the bathroom and dorm rooms before we leave. Then, we drop the blankets and dirty towels in a utility room downstairs. Before firing up the Bel Air, Kyle picks up one of the AAA maps and studies our route.

"Looks like we can skirt around the south edge of Kansas City," he says, "and barrel right on into Kansas."

"Let's go!" Annie says.

"Wait," I tell them. "This town's got a good vibe. Before we leave, let's hit a bank, see how we do with the half dollars."

Kyle glances at Annie in the back seat. She shrugs. "Fine with me."

We head back downtown and pull over at a bank on Holden.

"You got this covered?" Kyle asks me.

I stretch my hand back to Annie. "Money."

Annie slaps the thirty dollars into my palm. "Don't lose it."

Without dignifying that remark, I walk into the bank—another older, attractive building—and walk up to a pleasant-looking teller. A small nameplate on her counter reads "Naomi Williamson".

"May I help you?" she asks in a friendly voice.

I lay down the thirty dollars. "I was wondering if you have some half dollars I could buy."

She gives me a peculiar look, and I think *Uh-oh. Something's going on here.*

Immediately, I wonder if she somehow got a report on three runaways who are stopping at banks across the area. It seems unlikely, but I place my hand back on my money and prepare to flee.

Then, the teller says, "That's funny you should ask about half dollars."

"Why?" I croak.

"Well, just yesterday, a man came in and turned in a whole bunch of them."

I exhale. *Whew! They're not after us—at least, not yet.*

To the teller, I say, "Oh, is that right?"

Naomi opens a drawer and I see about twenty rolls of half dollars in brown paper wrappers. Then, I see something else. The wrappers have writing on them! And they look like dates!

I force myself to keep talking slowly. "Uh, I have thirty dollars. Could I buy three rolls?"

"You can have 'em all if you want. Not that many people use half dollars, and I'm glad to get rid of 'em."

"Uh, I only have enough cash for the three."

She picks up three of the rolls and takes my money. "Come back if you want the rest."

"I might do that."

Straining not to run, I hurry out the door and leap into the Bel Air.

"You get some?" Kyle asks.

"Yeah!"

He and Annie look at each other. "What's wrong?"

I look down at the wrappers and read the scribbled dates.

1951-D. 1955. 1943-D.

"Give me a roll," says Annie.

"Wait."

Carefully, I unfold the pressed-down end of the roll that says 1943-D and peer into it. Then, I do the same for the other rolls.

"Holy crap," I mutter.

"What is it?" Annie demands. "What's wrong?"

"Let me see," Kyle says, reaching for a roll.

"Careful. Don't take them out."

"*What?*" Annie repeats.

"These aren't regular half dollars," I finally explain. "I think they're *uncirculated* rolls of older halves."

"You mean they're 90% silver instead of 40%?" Annie asks.

Kyle grins. "Better 'n that, eh Mike? Uncirculated?"

"What's that mean?"

"It means they've never been used, and that they might be worth a whole lot more than just their silver value," I tell her.

"But why did the bank have them?" Kyle asks. "Have they just been sittin' there for the last, what, thirty years?"

"The teller says some old guy brought them in yesterday. He probably had them around his house for years and didn't know what he had."

"How much you think they're worth?"

"I don't know, but quick, drive back to the coin shop. The teller's got about seventeen more rolls in there. We need to sell these so we can come back and buy the rest before someone else grabs them."

By the time we go to the coin shop, sell the three rolls of half dollars, return to the bank and buy the rest of the rolls, then go *back* to the coin shop to sell *those* half dollars,

Kyle, Annie, and I are sitting on almost $600 cash.

"Wow," Kyle says, as we drive out of Warrensburg, "Anything like that ever happened to you before?"

I can't wipe the grin off of my face. "Not even close, but I've heard stories of other people striking it rich like that."

"Well, thank god for old fogies who hoard coins."

"Yeah. I only wish I could have kept some of the better ones."

Kyle pounds me on the back. "I know. Woulda made a nice collection. We appreciate your sacrifice."

After topping off the Bel Air with gas, we follow Highway 50 to Lee's Summit, Missouri, and then skirt the southern edge of Kansas City until we cross the state line into Kansas. The limestone and wooded hill country flattens out into farmland, and with cash in our pockets, we decide to splurge and stop for lunch at a diner in Lawrence. After we order, I step outside to buy today's *Kansas City Star* from a vending machine, and bring it back to the table.

"Gimme the comics," Annie says.

I find the right section and hand it to her.

I hold up the rest of the paper. "Kyle, you want any of this?"

He shakes his head and sips a cup of coffee, so I open the front section and start flipping through articles. I read an article about the aftermath of the fall of Saigon to North Vietnamese forces two months ago. Then an article about the continuing energy crisis.

Kyle glances over at me. "You really keep up with the news, dontcha?"

I shrug sheepishly. "A little, I guess. One of the bad

habits I picked up from my stepfather."

Kyle laughs, and I fold up the front section. I decide to open up the regional section next. I scan headlines about the state fair, a new downtown improvement project for Kansas City—nothing that interests me very much. Then, on page six, I find a column of news briefs.

My body freezes.

TWENTY-TWO

66 **U**h-oh."
Kyle is staring out the window, but hearing my tone of voice, snaps his head back toward me. Annie looks up from the comics.

"What?" she asks.

I glance all around to make sure no one is watching, then lay down the newspaper and silently point to a short paragraph. Kyle and Annie crane their necks to read it.

*** **Runaways Sought** ***

Authorities are seeking information on the whereabouts of three teenagers who disappeared from Birmingham, Alabama Wednesday afternoon. The two boys and a girl are driving a 1957 Bel Air with a Florida license plate. Their destination is uncertain, but appears to be Chicago or Denver. The three are not considered dangerous, but anyone with information about them should contact the Missouri State Patrol immediately.

A cloud descends over us.

"Oh, man," Kyle murmurs. "That ain't good."

"How do they know where we're goin'?" Annie hisses.

"They must have traced the phone call last night."

And then it hits me. "No," I tell them. "It's my fault."

"How can this be your fault?" Kyle asks, his eyes still on the article.

"The Triple-A office in Jefferson City. I specifically asked for a map of Denver."

His eyes meet mine. "Mike, you didn't."

"Annie was right there."

"Shoot. That's right," she says. "It was that mean woman. She musta called somebody soon as we left."

I tell them, "It didn't even occur to me at the time what a stupid thing that was. I'm sorry, you guys. I should have just headed back on the bus from Birmingham."

Kyle runs his hand through his hair, and quickly taps his knuckles on the tabletop. "No," he says. "Anyone woulda done the same. It ain't your fault."

I appreciate him trying to make me feel better, but think, *Mike, you really screwed up this time.*

Kyle quickly surveys the room for eavesdroppers, and then leans in close. "Okay, look. We're still alright. Hardly no one's gonna read that little item in the newspaper. I doubt it's even gone out to most police and sheriff's stations."

"You don't think so?" Annie asks.

"Naw. Listen, you know how many runaways there are in this country? Hundreds. More 'n that. *Thousands.* Police got better things to do 'n worry about every dang one."

I rub my hands slowly over my face and try to think clearly. Part of what Kyle's saying makes sense. *On the other hand, most runaways don't ever make it into newsprint. If this newspaper printed the report, maybe the Authorities—whoever they are—are looking for us pretty hard.*

"Let's stay calm," Kyle says. "Just finish up our lunch like we ain't got a care. Then, we high-tail it outta here."

"To where?" I ask.

"To Denver, of course!"

"You still want to go to Denver when we know they might be waiting for us there?"

"We'll stick to back roads," Kyle says. "Now that we got maps, we can just pick smaller routes where we ain't likely to run into any state troopers."

"But why Denver?" I ask. "We could head straight north, or south—anywhere where they're not looking for us."

"And miss out on that silver dollar?"

I sit back in my seat. "You're not still thinking about *that*?"

"I'm *especially* thinkin' of it now. Look, Mike," he says, and I again lean closer. "If Annie and me go to Canada—"

"I *ain't* goin' to Canada," Annie blurts.

Kyle slowly looks at her and sighs. "*Wherever* we go, we're gonna need money. A boatload of it. We're not gonna get that swappin' out silver half dollars or even me getting' a job for five bucks an hour."

"I can work," Annie says.

"You're only thirteen."

"But, I can pass for sixteen, seventeen if I have to."

"Annie, will you just shut up for a minute?"

"Fine." Annie's lower lip juts out.

"So like I was sayin'," Kyle continues. "We're gonna need money. That Peace dollar could be our ticket to someplace else."

"But Kyle, you don't even know if we can find one."

"We'll find one."

I'm about to object further, but our waitress brings us our lunch.

After we finish wolfing down our sandwiches, fries,

and Cokes, we resume our conversation.

"Kyle," I say, "if they think we're going to Denver, the authorities there will definitely be looking for us!"

"I know," Kyle says. "But in a big city like that, it'll be a whole lot easier to lose ourselves. We can ditch the Bel Air, ride buses. While we're lookin' for the Peace dollar, we can even split up. Believe me, Mike, no one's even gonna raise an eyebrow."

"But what if we don't find the Peace dollar?"

Kyle shrugs. "Then, we don't find it. Annie and me keep movin' and you go back to Pensacola. Simple as that."

"How far is it to Denver?" Annie asks.

"I think it's about six hundred miles," I tell her. "Six hundred miles of wide-open *exposed* countryside where it's easy to spot an old, souped-up hot rod."

Kyle grins. "Well, then, I guess we'll just have to drive really, really *fast*."

TWENTY-THREE

A nd that's exactly what we do.

Leaving Lawrence, we navigate a series of two-lane state and county roads that take us through small towns and farmland. The farther from Kansas City we drive, the less traffic we encounter and, as promised, Kyle takes the leash off the Bel Air.

"This is more like it!" Annie yells as Kyle presses down on the accelerator.

I look over at the speedometer and see the needle climb to ninety miles per hour. The engine purrs like it's barely straining.

"I'd go even faster, except I gotta keep an eye out for guys pullin' onto the road with tractors and stuff," Kyle explains over the roar of air rushing through the open windows.

Indeed, all around us fields sway with corn and other crops I don't recognize. Farmers are hard at work, using tractors to move irrigation lines, fertilize fields, and do, well, *farmer things* that farmers do. Every ten or twenty miles, we're forced to slow down for towns like McPherson and Lyons, but throughout the afternoon we eat up the Kansas map, one distant water tower at a time. By the time we pick up U.S. 50 again west of Hutchison, we've left the lusher eastern half of the state and enter dry, rolling grasslands.

Amazingly, we see only one patrol car the entire afternoon. Kyle spots it way ahead of time and slows the Bel Air to the legal limit. We all hold our breaths as we pass the black-and-white, but the officer only gives us a glance.

We reach Dodge City about dinnertime, but decide it's too risky to sit in a restaurant again. Kyle drops me off at a grocery store while he and Annie go fill up with gas and check the Bel Air's oil and tires. I stock up on bread, baloney, Cheetos, Twinkies, and other essential food groups. When I emerge from the store, the Bel Air is waiting for me.

"You're in my seat," I tell Annie, who's now riding shotgun.

She seizes the bag of Cheetos and tears it open. "I was just bein' nice lettin' you have it before."

"Don't get too comfortable. I want it back."

After crawling into the back seat, I pull out the loaf of bread, and some cheese and baloney. "Kyle," I say, "isn't Dodge City where they used to drive longhorn cattle up from Texas to ship them east by train?"

"Sounds right," he answers, reaching over for a handful of Cheetos from Annie. "Seems like a lot of the old T.V. westerns were always takin' place here. Every episode, cowboys and marshals were gunnin' each other down with their six-shooters."

"That's right! I think Wyatt Earp was a lawman here."

"I don' know about that, but I think we're gonna be lucky to 'get outta Dodge'."

"You guys are nuts," Annie tells us, and Kyle and I both crack up.

One thing's for sure—this part of Kansas is still cattle country. In Dodge City and later, in Garden City, we pass stockyards with acres and acres of penned-up cattle right next to huge meat-packing plants.

"Look at all them cows!" Kyle says, munching a

cheese-and-baloney sandwich I've made him.

"There must be thousands of them," I say.

"More. Tens 'a thousands."

Annie is also eating a baloney sandwich. "Pee-ew!" she exclaims as thick clouds of manure-and-cow smell pour into the Bel Air.

"Don't complain," I say. "Where do you think the meat in that sandwich comes from?"

Annie stares at her baloney. "You mean, they kill them poor cows?"

"Every one of 'em," Kyle answers, taking an especially big bite of his sandwich and holding his mouth open for Annie to see.

"Gross!" Annie cries, and tosses the rest of her sandwich out the window. "I'm gonna be a vegetarian."

Past Garden City, it's only another fifty miles to the Colorado border.

"Looks like we're going to make it," I say.

Kyle nods. "Looks like, but this road's too big. Too exposed. Anythin' smaller we can take?"

I open up the Kansas map for the tenth time today, "There's not too many farm roads around, but up here at Syracuse, you can turn north onto 27. That looks like it's a lot smaller, and it'll take us to Tribune, where we can head west again into Colorado."

"Sounds good."

And it is, for a while. We cover the thirty-four miles between Syracuse and Tribune in twenty-five minutes. In Tribune, a one grocery-store town with maybe a thousand people in it, we turn west for the last dash to Colorado.

"State line 18 miles!" Annie reads, as Kyle runs the

Bel Air through its gears.

I also feel my spirits lift. "Colorado, here we come!"

Kyle looks in his rearview mirror. "Well, maybe not quite yet."

"*What?*"

I spin around to see familiar red-and-blue flashing lights about half a mile back. My liver leaps into my throat.

"What are you going to do?"

"You can't stop!" Annie pleads.

"I ain't fixin' to. Buckle up!"

The sudden acceleration of the Bel Air throws me into the back of the seat, and I frantically search for a seat belt.

"There *aren't* any seatbelts back here!"

Kyle doesn't glance back. "It was just a, whaddya say, figure of speech."

"Thanks."

The Bel Air engine roars and the patrol car's siren leaps to life behind us.

"You think it's police or state troopers?" I shout to Kyle.

"Probably just the county sheriff, but I ain't fixin' to find out!"

The road runs straight and flat, and I feel the Bel Air stretch out like a cheetah. Unfortunately, the patrol car shows no sign of giving up.

"Is he gainin'?" Annie yells to me.

"Doesn't look like it, but we're not losing him either! How fast are we going?"

"110!"

"Can we go any faster?"

Without answering, Kyle presses down harder on the accelerator, and I watch the needle climb past 115, 120, up to 125. I grow breathless watching it. Before meeting up with Kyle again, the fastest I've ever gone in a car is probably 80—and that was when my stepfather drove too fast by accident.

"How're we doin', Mike?" Kyle calls back.

I again spin around. "He's still with us!"

"Oh, he's *not!*" Kyle yells, indignant. "Who does he think he's drivin' against?"

With his jaw set, Kyle keeps pushing the Bel Air to 130, 135 miles per hour.

"Do you think he knows who we are?" Annie yells.

"I sure hope not!"

"He's falling back!" I yell.

"Finally!"

Just then, I see a "Welcome to Colorado" sign streak by our headlights.

"He's still falling back!"

Kyle eases off of the gas pedal and lets the speed drift down, checking the rearview mirror to make sure the patrol car isn't following.

"He probably didn't want to cross the state line," I say. "Do you think he called ahead to the cops on this side of the border?"

"Likely," Kyle says. "Mike, can you get us off 'a this road?"

"Just a minute. Where's the light switch?"

Kyle reaches down next to the steering wheel to turn on the dome light, and I open the Colorado map for the first time.

"There's a dirt road coming up."

"See it!"

Kyle brakes and swings off onto a road that's actually

gravel, not dirt, and starts driving north.

"You think they're gonna look for us?" Annie asks.

"Don' know," her brother answers.

"It probably depends on if they know who we are or not," I add. "That patrol car was far enough back, I'm not sure he could tell we were in a Bel Air. If he was just after us for speeding, I wouldn't think they'd put too much effort into trying to catch us. Do you think we should find a place to pull over for a while?"

"How far is it to Denver?" Kyle asks.

I again check the map.

"Well, if we pick up U.S. 40 about thirty miles ahead, and take it to Interstate 70, looks like about 200 miles. If we stay on these back roads, it's going to be farther."

"But close enough we can get there before sunrise?"

"You wanna drive all night again?" Annie complains.

"No," Kyle admits. "But it's gonna be a heck of a lot safer, dontcha think, Mike?"

"Probably. People won't see us as easily, and there won't be as many officers on duty, either. Are you tired? You want me to drive for a while?"

Kyle chuckles. "After that little race, I got enough juice flowin' through me to drive to Alaska."

I laugh. "Okay, but just tell me when you want me to start ruining the Bel Air's transmission again. And Annie, get out of my seat!"

TWENTY-FOUR

Annie does finally switch seats with me—but only because she wants to hit the sack. Like Kyle, I have too much adrenaline to even think about sleep. Between car chases and worrying about getting pulled over and thinking that I really ought to be back in Florida with my dad, I feel like I've gulped down several gallons of coffee— or the pure caffeine equivalent.

"Do we have enough gas to make it all the way to Denver?" I ask Kyle.

He studies the fuel gauge. "Pretty close, but that high-speed sprint didn't do nothin' for our mileage. Neither do these gravel roads."

"I just think they're safer than any other routes."

"I hear ya."

Using the map to guide us, we slowly zigzag our way north and west, through a mixture of farmland and rough, rolling plateau country. It makes for a long night, but it's worth it when we finally see dawn cast a pink glow to Pike's Peak, and the Rocky Mountain Front in the distance.

"So that's what real mountains look like," Kyle murmurs.

Being from California, I've seen plenty of mountains before, but I catch Kyle's sense of wonder looking at the dramatic uplift and buckling of the earth on the horizon.

Though it's early, traffic picks up as we approach Denver, and we decide to risk linking back up with U.S. 40, which turns into a large street called East Colfax that arrows toward town. Going down a little hill past Chambers Road, we catch our first good view of the high-rises of downtown Denver, seven or eight miles away. The Rockies, much closer now, form a dramatic backdrop to the city, and I can feel my excitement grow.

By now, the Bel Air is running on fumes so Kyle stops at one of those new self-service gas stations where you have to pump the gas yourself. While Kyle fills the tank, I use the restroom and then dig out the Colorado tour book I got from our favorite AAA office in Jefferson City, MO. As I'm flipping pages, a steady procession of commercial jets roar overhead—traffic from Denver's Stapleton Airport, only a mile or two away.

When Kyle returns from paying for the gas and using the restroom himself, he glances back at Annie, still crashed in the back seat. "We gotta find us a place to hole up and get some rest," he says.

"According to this book, Colfax Avenue here might be our best bet. The lodging locator map shows motels strung all along it. "

"Works for me." Kyle starts up the Bel Air again and we pull out, heading toward downtown.

I've seen a lot of "strips" in different cities before, but right away, I can tell I've never seen anything like this. Colfax Avenue is mile after mile of restaurants, liquor stores, car dealerships, auto parts stores, pawnshops, bars, gas stations, strip malls, strip *clubs*—you name it, Colfax has got it. Fortunately for us, a lot of it isn't exactly what you'd call "high class". We pass numerous, cheapy motels with lofty names like the Manor House, Top-Star, Riviera, and Biltmore. Others appeal to travelers looking for a Wild West theme—motels like the Timberline, Ranger, Branding Iron, Lazy C, and Ahwanee. My favorite is a two-story place called the Niagara Falls Motel.

Kyle snorts. "Mike, I think you steered us in the wrong direction. You didn't tell us we were goin' to New York."

Several of the motels offer weekly rates and kitchenettes—just the ticket for three fugitives on a budget. We drive by several more possibilities before passing a brick motel called the Cottonwood.

"How about that one?" Kyle asks.

"Looks good to me."

He pulls a quick U-turn and drives around behind the motel, next to a dumpster, so that the Bel Air can't be spotted from Colfax.

Finally, Annie stirs and sits up. "What time is it? Is this Denver?"

"Stay here," Kyle tells us. "I want the manager to think it's just me needin' a room."

He disappears around to the front of the motel, and I ask Annie, "How'd you sleep?"

"Okay, considerin' I was sleepin' in a car all night. Those roads jostled me around like a rock tumbler."

"Safer to take the back roads," I tell her.

"I gotta pee bad."

"Kyle's getting us a room."

"Good."

A few minutes later, he returns and tosses me a key. "Room 12. It's out of eyesight of the office. You two go to the room. I'm gonna park the Bel Air down a side street."

We grab our stuff and hurry inside to find two sagging double beds that look like they've been used as trampolines. Along with the other usual amenities, the room has a refrigerator, a cupboard, and a sink for doing dishes.

The place smells a little funky, but we're too tired to care.

"How much did this set us back?" I ask when Kyle returns.

"Talked him down to $85 for the week."

"I'd a given him fifty," Annie grumbles.

"Well next time you can do the negotiatin'," Kyle snaps at her.

We polish off the rest of our groceries from Dodge City before brushing our teeth and getting ready to crash on the beds.

"I ain't sharin' a bed with either of you two stinky guys," Annie says.

"Yes, you are," Kyle says. "We wouldn't even have a room if it wasn't for Mike's idea with the half dollars. Annie, you 'n me are takin' this one. Mike you get your own."

I don't object. As open-minded as I like to think I am, the thought of sharin' a bed with Kyle, well…

We snore away the rest of the morning and most of the afternoon. At least some of us do. When I wake up and glance over at the other bed, I see that Kyle is the only occupant. I get up and check the bathroom.

No Annie.

I am just about to put my shoes on to go look for her, when she sneaks quietly back into the room.

"Where have you been?"

"Wasn't sleepy," she says. "Thought I'd go look around. Mike, did you see them mountains?"

I ignore her question, and glance over at Kyle to make sure he's still sawing logs. "Annie, are you sure that's such a good idea, walking around like that?"

"Whaddya mean?"

"I mean they're looking for us—and you especially. What if a policeman picked you up?"

"Nobody did. Besides, ain't no one gonna recognize me without you two."

"Uh, I don't know about that. Your aunt and uncle probably gave photographs to the police. I just think you should check with Kyle and me before you go off by yourself."

Even though she's thirteen, she sticks her lip out. "You're not my daddy."

I'm getting a little tired of her selfishness. "Fine," I tell her, my voice tightening. "Do what you want and get sent back to Alabama. It'll serve you right."

Annie doesn't say anything for a moment. Then, she sits down on the bed next to me. When she speaks again, her attitude is gone and her voice is quiet. "I don't wanna go back to Alabama."

I see the worry on her face and regret my choice of words. "Pretty bad, huh?"

"You don' know," she says. "My aunt and uncle started in on me the moment I got there. Said I didn't have no manners and didn't know how to work. They were on my case every second."

"That must have been rough."

"It was *awful*. When I started makin' friends, they wouldn't let me do anything with 'em. Said they weren't the 'right sort' I should be hangin' out with. I used to sneak out anyway, but one time, my uncle caught me, and they grounded me for a whole month. It got so's I could hardly breathe."

She pauses and I have to admit, I am surprised she's talking to me. *I guess she needs to talk about it with somebody,*

I think, and try to keep the conversation going.

"Your uncle's a preacher?"

A disdainful sound rises from her throat. "He calls himself that, but he just gets up and tries to scare everyone about goin' to hell."

"Did they make you go to church?"

"At first, but then I told 'em I wasn't goin' no more."

I raise my eyebrows. "What did they do?"

"Couldn't do much. They'd already grounded me, but my aunt stayed back to make sure I wasn't sneakin' out."

I wait a moment, and then ask. "When did your uncle start, you know, going after you?"

"Huh?" Annie looks at me for a second, and at first, I think that maybe I've stepped into unwanted territory. On the other hand, she really looks like she doesn't understand what I asked, so I rephrase the question.

I point to the bruise on her cheek. "You know, uh, when did he start hitting you?"

Recognition flashes in her eyes and she raises her hand to her face.

Her reaction confuses me. *Isn't that the main reason she was so desperate to get away from them?* I think, but before I can ponder it more, she says, "That just started a few weeks ago."

Just then, Kyle rolls over. "What's all the jabberin' about?"

"Nothing," I tell him. "Annie and I were just talking."

"What time is it?"

Over the sink hangs a little hexagonal clock with tiny tiles surrounding it. I remember having one just like it in our apartment before my parents got divorced.

"Three o'clock."

"Maybe we should go get us a look at the Mint before it closes," Kyle suggests.

"The Mint is open on Saturday?" Annie asks.

My head snaps toward her. "It's Saturday? I thought it was Friday."

"Me, too," Kyle admits. "Time flies when you're on the run. So what y'all wanna do?"

"There's a bowling alley down the street," Annie says.

"How ya know that?" Kyle asks.

"I went out for a while."

Kyle sits up. "Annie! What were you thinkin'?"

I look over at Annie and make an "I told you so" face.

She grabs a pillow and clutches it in front of her. "I wasn't hurtin' nobody! Geez, both of you are so uptight."

"I already told her she shouldn't go out alone," I explain.

"Mike's right, Annie. Don't pull any more stunts like that, or we're all gonna end up in jail."

"Speaking of that," I say. "I should call my dad. I think I was supposed to call him yesterday."

"Better use a pay phone," Kyle says.

I empty my pockets. "I don't have enough change. Either of you have any?"

Between us, we scrounge up a couple bucks in quarters and dimes.

"I'll be back," I tell them.

"Be careful," Kyle says.

TWENTY-FIVE

Kyle's warning sinks in as I leave the motel. In the late afternoon, Colfax Avenue seems even seedier than in the morning. People stand around on street corners, not doing anything, but carefully eyeing anyone passing by. While I wait to cross one street, a guy comes up to me and asks, "Hey man, you want to buy some grass?"

"No thanks."

"I got other stuff, too."

I keep walking.

A block later, I pass a group of three women who seem overdressed for the neighborhood and time of day. One of them calls, "Hey, Baby. You want some company?"

I halt, and my mouth opens in surprise as my brain figures out that the women just might want to be paid for my companionship. Seeing my expression, the three women burst into laughter and I hurry down the sidewalk.

"Come back and see us, Sugar Plum!" a voice yells after me.

I finally find a phone booth next to a pawnshop a couple blocks farther on. As I shut myself inside, I feel a little safer, but this is not a call I'm looking forward to. I've already been gone four days and am supposed to be heading back to Florida now. Even as I pick up the receiver I'm not sure what I'm going to say to my dad, or how he's going to react.

I take a deep breath and dial '0' for operator. I've decided not to make a collect call because I figure that might be traced more easily, but I really don't know anything about the World of Tracing Phone Calls.

"Operator. What city?"

"Pensacola, Florida."

After being transferred, I give a second operator the phone number, put in the coins, and wait for the phone to ring.

My dad picks up on the third ring.

"Hello?"

"Dad, it's me."

"Son, am I glad to hear from you! I thought you'd call earlier."

"I'm sorry. I didn't have a chance."

"Why not? Are you on your way home?"

Well, I think, *at least he hasn't seen any reports of the three runaways yet.*

"Uh, not exactly."

His voice grows concerned. "Why? What's going on? Are you okay?"

"Yeah. We're all fine."

"All? I thought it was just Kyle and you?"

Darn! I didn't mean to let slip that Annie was with us.

"Uh, it is," I stammer.

"Mike, I don't like this. You sound like you're in trouble."

"No, not really. It's just, uh, I'm going to need a couple more days. There was some stuff Kyle and I wanted to see," I say, my mind groping for a convincing story, "and the Bel Air's having some mechanical problems."

"What kind of mechanical problems?"

Already feeling guilty for the lies, I say, "I don't know. Something about the cooling. Kyle could tell you."

"Do you need me to wire you some money?"

"No…thanks."

"Where are you, then?"

"Um…I'm not exactly sure."

"Mike, listen," my dad says, "I know it's been different this year with the baby and Paula and everything. I probably didn't realize how hard that would be on you."

You got that right.

"But," my dad continues, "I really want you back home. Your mom called and I didn't know what to tell her. I made up a story about you visiting a friend, but that's not going to fly the next time."

"Is that the only reason you want me home? So you don't have to explain anything to my mother?" My words come out angrier than I realize.

"No, of course not. I miss you, son. We *all* miss you. Even David looks for you."

I grunt.

"Seriously, son. You need to get on a bus and just head home. If Kyle needs money to fix his car, I'll be happy to help him out, but you need to get back here."

"I can't…not right away," I tell him. "I wouldn't feel right."

Just then, the operator cuts in. "Please deposit $1.35 to continue your call."

I seize the opportunity to say, "Dad, I have to go. Just a couple more days, okay?"

"Mike—"

The line clicks off and I hang up the receiver.

I take another big breath and let it out slowly.

"Well, that went well," I mutter to myself, flinging open the phone booth door.

When I get back to the room, Kyle has showered and

is shaving in front of the bathroom sink, wearing a towel around his waist.

"Put some clothes on," Annie tells him. "Mike and I don' wanna stare at your ugly back."

"I ain't got any clean clothes," Kyle answers.

"Neither do Mike 'n me," Annie says. "That doesn't mean we gotta walk around naked."

"We need to do some laundry," Kyle says, then looks at me in the mirror. "How'd it go with your dad?"

"Not great, but I think I bought a couple more days."

Kyle puts down his razor and turns to me. "He know anything about what's goin' on?"

I shake my head. "Not yet, but it's only a matter of time."

"Well, I guess that's good. Means not every part of the country is lookin' for us."

"I guess." Then, to change the subject, I say, "What do you say we try to find a coin shop before closing time?"

"What for?" Annie says. "We ain't got no more half dollars."

"I know, but I thought a local guy might know something about the Peace dollars."

"Sounds good to me," Kyle says.

Annie throws a pillow at him. "Get dressed!"

I pull the phone book from underneath the room phone and turn to the "Coin Shop" listings in the Yellow Pages.

"Got anything to write with?" I ask Kyle and Annie.

"Just tear the page out," says Kyle.

"Someone else might want to use it."

Kyle looks at me impatiently. "Mike, it's a *phone book*. They make a new one every year. Besides, how many people staying here are gonna look up a coin shop?"

I keep searching for a pen and paper when Annie seizes the phone book and rips out the page. "See, Mike? It just takes practice."

Kyle laughs.

After leaving the motel, we walk three blocks through back streets to the Bel Air.

"I didn't know where else to park it," Kyle says. "None of this area looks too safe."

"Half a dozen people offered to sell me drugs while I was looking for a phone," I tell him.

Kyle looks at me. "That right?"

"Well, not half a dozen."

Kyle turns to his sister. "That does it, Annie. Don't go anywhere without us, you hear?"

"Jesus, I heard y'all the first time!"

We climb into the Bel Air and make our way back to Colfax, heading downtown. As we drive, the buildings get taller, and we start to feel more like we're in a real city.

"Look, there's the Capitol," I say, pointing to a spectacular golden dome up ahead. "According to this map, the Mint's right on the other side."

"You want me to keep goin' straight?" Kyle asks.

"No. Turn left on Broadway. The phone book lists a couple of coin shops down that way."

By now, the traffic is heavier, and the Bel Air blends in with a lot of other older cars driving around. About two miles down Broadway, Annie yells, "I see it. Mountain Coins."

Broadway is a one-way street, so Kyle pulls over to the left curb in front of the store. We pile out and enter one of the largest coin shops I've ever been in. Instead of just one or two banks of display cases, the store is divided into different sections, each with its own experts working there.

Annie wanders over to a case full of half dollars and starts fiddling with the buttons to make it spin around. Meanwhile, Kyle and I approach a sign that says "Silver Dollars".

A man looks up at us. Even though he's miles from the nearest dude ranch, he wears a Western-style plaid shirt and a cowboy hat.

His horse must be parked out back, I think.

The man smiles and says, "What can I do for you?"

Kyle looks at me with a nod.

"I was just wondering what you might know about the 1964 Peace dollars?"

The question stops the man. "You mean the silver dollars they melted down?"

"Yeah, those."

The man frowns a bit. "Why do you want to know?"

"Oh," I explain. "We read that article in this month's *Coin Universe*. We both thought it was interesting and figured that since we're in Denver, people here might know more about it."

The man's face relaxes and he straightens his already-straight cowboy hat. "I see. Well, I'm afraid I can't tell you much of anything other than what's in the article."

"Do you think any still exist?"

"Shoot, who knows? I mean, there are rumors."

"You ever seen one of 'em?" Kyle asks.

The man's jaw clenches, and then he forces a laugh. "Oh, sure."

"Really?"

"Sure. Hundreds. Every day."

"Oh," I say, picking up the sarcasm.

"In fact, you got any you'd like to sell?" The man's clearly enjoying himself now.

"No. Thank you for your time."

Kyle and I are about to turn away, when I stop and reach into my pocket. I pull out the "Love Dollar" Annie discovered back in Missouri and hand it to the man.

"Say, have you ever seen one of these before?"

The man takes the token by the edges and looks at it. "Now *this*, I can tell you about. Where'd you find it?"

"We pulled it out of a half dollar roll," I tell him, careful not to mention *where*.

"Huh. Well, these are minted by a guy named Dan Carroll right here in Denver. Dan's a coin collector who used to work at the Mint. He got let go for some reason and decided to start making his own coins."

"Is that legal?" I ask.

"Oh, they're not real coins. Just tokens like this one. I like a lot of them. He's got a good sense of humor and he parodies some real coins. Some people hate what he's doing, but he's got a collector following, and people bring them in or ask for them from time to time."

"They worth anything?" Kyle asks.

"If you collect them, they are. This one's just made out of copper and nickel, so it's probably not worth much, but he makes some in silver, too."

"By the way," the man says, returning the token to me. "If you're really interested in those Peace dollars, Dan would be a person to talk to. I think he was working at the Mint when they made them."

"Do you know where we can find him?"

"Let me see." He turns away and starts flipping through one of those little Rolodex file systems that people keep addresses and phone numbers on. He pulls out a card and scribbles the address on a piece of paper.

"He calls himself the Mile-High Mint."

"Okay," I say, taking the paper. "Thanks."

TWENTY-SIX

The next day is a drag. Really. It's Sunday so the Mint is closed. We try calling Dan Carroll, but he doesn't answer his phone. Annie wants to drive around, see the sights, but Kyle and I squash the idea.

"That Bel Air ain't exactly a Ford Pinto," Kyle tells Annie. "Someone could easily recognize it."

"And the three of us together stick out, too," I add. "Especially on a Sunday when there aren't so many people around."

"I don't care," Annie huffs. "I ain't gonna sit in this stupid room all day. I wanna get out, and do somethin'."

"No," Kyle tells her.

"Yes!"

"Why don't you read a book?" Kyle asks, changing tactics. "You used to read all the time."

"I ain't got no book!"

"You can read mine," I say, holding up the copy of *Mila 18* I brought with me.

"No thanks," Annie says, scrunching up her nose.

And that's pretty much how the whole day goes. We watch bad television. Kyle and Annie fight. We take naps. Kyle and Annie fight. We wash out clothes in the sink. Kyle and Annie—well, they fight.

Just to quit listening to them, I go out and get us some hamburgers for lunch. Along the way, I pick up a *Denver Post*. While we chew on our burgers and fries, the three of us comb every section of the paper, looking to see if we're in it. Fortunately, we don't find a thing, not in the news or in the police reports.

"That's a break at least," I say. "Maybe they've stopped looking for us."

"Maybe," Kyle says.

"Can we go out now?" Annie whines.

Kyle and I both turn to her and shout "No!"

In the late afternoon, though, Kyle does step out. He doesn't say where he's going, but gives Annie clear instructions to stay put.

"Don't go *anywhere*, Annie. Not even down the street."

"I *hate* you!" she shouts, hurling a Kleenex box at him.

Kyle lets it bounce off of his shoulder, but looks at me as if to say, "Make sure she doesn't leave."

It's not a task I'm looking forward to, but I nod.

Surprisingly, Annie doesn't try to sneak away. Instead, she finds the comics section of the paper and sits pouting on her bed.

"I hate this place," she says. "There's nothin' to do and my stupid brother won't let us go nowhere."

I don't want to get in the middle of their squabble, but feel I should defend Kyle. "He's just looking out for you. If they *have* put out a bulletin, you could easily get picked up and sent back."

Annie doesn't seem to hear me. "And this room is the pits. Somethin' was bitin' me last night. I think the beds got bedbugs in 'em."

"Really?" I look up from the sports section. "I woke up with a few bites, but I thought they were from mosquitoes. What do bedbugs look like?"

"They're—" Annie begins, then exclaims, "Ooh, *yuck*. There's one on the wall!"

"What?"

I don't believe her, so I walk over to where she's pointing. Sure enough, an ugly red creature about half as big as my little fingernail is crawling up the wallpaper.

"Kill it," she says.

I grab the Kleenex box and smash it. Blood squirts out from its fat little body.

"Gross," I mutter.

"Told ya."

Without thinking, I start scratching my arms and legs all over, even where I don't have any bites. Suddenly, I'm feeling just as eager as Annie to get out of here, but instead of admitting it, I say, "Tomorrow will be better. There will be more people on the streets, and we'll be able to see if there's any chance of us finding one of the Peace dollars."

"What if we don't?"

"Well, then, you and Kyle better high-tail it out of here, and I'll hop a bus back to Florida."

Annie looks over at me. "Do ya think they'll find us, Mike?"

I am still scratching and scanning the wall for more bedbugs, but pause long enough to meet her eyes. "I doubt it," I tell her. "Not if you keep heading west, and stay out of sight."

Annie nods. "I just wanna get as far away as possible."

That night, I toss and turn like a dog with fleas. Between thinking about bedbugs and worrying about our situation, my brain refuses to power down. When I finally do doze for a few hours, I start dreaming about being attacked by thousands of hungry red insects, and wake up scratching like crazy. I open my eyes to see a dim light showing around the edge of the curtains.

"I give up," I mutter, surrendering the sleep battle once and for all.

I decide I might as well shave and take a shower—and examine myself for bites. I find three or four new ones, but when I step out of the bathroom, I discover I wasn't the only one tossing and turning. Kyle and Annie are also up, just as eager as I am to get moving.

Kyle decides we should avoid using the Bel Air as much as possible, so we walk to a nearby McDonald's for Egg McMuffins, and then catch a city bus straight down Colfax to the U.S. Mint. We're about the only white faces on the bus, but we don't get more than a glance from the other passengers. Most seem like they're heading to work downtown, thinking about the day and minding their own business.

After passing the state capitol building and the Denver City and County Building, Kyle pulls the "STOP" cord and the bus pulls over right across the street from the Mint. We arrive just in time for the first tour of the day, at 8:00 a.m.

The Mint is a neat stone building, and looks like it was built a long time ago. It's only two tall stories high, but stretches about a block long and a narrow block wide—still tiny compared to the other government buildings nearby. We join a small line of tourists waiting under a long cloth awning and soon, a tour guide escorts all of us into the building and up some stairs to the mezzanine level.

The history of the Denver Mint, we soon learn, began with Clark, Gruber, & Company, after gold was discovered in Colorado in 1858. Clark and Gruber were two business partners who took advantage of Denver's remote location to start their own banking company, independent of the U.S. government. They took in gold dust and nuggets, melted them down, and minted their own private gold coins that were used by Colorado miners, businessmen, and residents.

"In 1862," our guide explains, "an Act of Congress allowed the U.S. government to buy the Clark-Gruber facility and turn it into an assay office for weighing and measuring gold. For several decades, however, no U.S. coins were minted here in Denver. Even after construction of the building we're standing in now, from 1897 to 1904, delays kept coins from being produced here until 1906. At that time, the Mint finally began turning out coins with the "D" mintmark on them."

Being a coin nut, I am fascinated with everything the woman is saying. I look over at Annie, though, and see her fiddling with her blonde hair, already bored three minutes into the tour. Kyle seems more interested, but keeps reaching for his pack of cigarettes before remembering that no smoking is allowed in the building. I can't tell if he's also bored, or just anxious to see if we can learn anything about the Peace dollars.

A bank of windows lines one side of the room we're standing in and, after giving us the history of the place, the tour guide steps over to the windows to show us an enormous work floor below us. Suddenly, Kyle and Annie perk up. From our glass-enclosed viewpoint, we see an assortment of giant machines for making coin blanks. The process is a lot more complicated than I would have expected. Massive ingots of copper and nickel are rolled into thin sheets, some almost a mile long, before coin blanks are punched out of them by another machine. The blanks are cleaned, heated, and rolled to give them rims, before being inspected and sent on to another department.

Speaking of other departments, from the first room, our tour guide ushers us down a hallway to more glass windows. These look down on a room full of coin presses—the actual machines that stamp out the coins. The windows here don't reach all the way to the ceiling, so the loud clatter of machines fills our ears, but we hardly notice. Instead, our attention is fixed on the thousands of pennies, dimes, nickels, and quarters spilling out into giant bins below us.

"Wow," I murmur.

"Wish we could get us some of those," Annie quips.

As we watch, I see a man walk over to a bin of pennies that's almost full. He picks up a couple and examines them with an eyeglass. Then, he tosses them back into the bin, and motions for another worker to come collect them with a little vehicle that looks like a forklift.

Our tour guide tells us, "That man there will haul the pennies over to other machines for counting and bagging. Then, they will be stored or shipped to our nation's Federal Reserve banks, ready to enter our money supply."

Just then, Kyle raises his hand, and asks, "Ma'am, can you tell us anything about the 1964 silver dollars y'all made here?"

A trace of annoyance flickers across the tour guide's face, but she quickly recovers and begins recounting the same story we read in my copy of the *Coin Universe*. Kyle's question, though, has attracted the attention of other people on the tour, and they crowd in closer to listen.

"Could any of the dollars still exist?" a man next to me asks.

The tour guide's voice tightens. "No. Every single one of the silver dollars was destroyed after minting."

"Could anyone, you know, sneak some of the coins out of the Mint?" asks a girl about our age.

Our guide seems to puff out her chest. "Absolutely not. Strict guidelines are in place to ensure that any coins made in the facility stay in the facility unless they are released by official procedures. Do you see those men over there?" she asks, pointing to two uniformed men with badges. "Those are members of the Mint Police, a special police force that makes doubly sure our nation's coinage—*your* coinage—is fully protected."

Satisfied that she has defended the Mint's honor and reputation, the guide says, "Now, if you'll just follow—"

"Excuse me," I interrupt. "Just one more question. Which of the machines here were used to make those 1964 dollars?"

The guide looks at me, exasperated. "I'm really not sure," she answers. "Now, if you'll all just keep walking this way."

Kyle and I glance at each other, and I can see by his face that he's thinking what I am. *She either doesn't know, or she doesn't want to tell us.*

As we're leaving the glass hallway to wrap up the tour, however, I happen to glance down at a coin press that is punching out quarters, and I see something interesting occur. It happens so fast that I hardly have time to think about it, but it lodges in my brain just the same...

TWENTY-SEVEN

O ur entire Mint tour lasts only fifteen minutes. The highlight is a stop by a giant vault that contains six massive ingots of solid gold. The tour guide explains that while Fort Knox stores most of our nation's gold supply, a good portion of it resides here at the Denver Mint. As an added bonus, she hands us all shiny new Bicentennial quarters, which are being minted by the millions even though it isn't 1976 quite yet.

"Cool," Annie says, turning the coin over in her hands.

Before we can ask any more questions, though, the Mint guide herds us to the end of the hall, down some steps, and into the Mint gift shop. After we spill back onto Delaware Street, Kyle says, "Well, that was interestin'."

"Yeah," I say, as we start walking back toward the bus stop, "but not very helpful."

"They don't seem much interested in talkin' about the '64 Peace dollars."

"I didn't really expect them to. Remember the *Coin Universe* article? It said the Mint didn't even admit they'd made the cartwheels until years later. They're probably still embarrassed the story got out."

"Hmm..." Kyle muses. "Maybe we should come on back here when this shift of workers gets out. Ask if anyone knows anythin' more?"

"I'm hungry," Annie says.

Kyle grabs Annie in a playful headlock. "Annie, we just had breakfast! How can you be hungry again already?"

"Ow! Let me go!"

Kyle releases her, and she punches him in the shoulder.

"You know," I say, "I looked at a map last night. That Dan guy, who has that Mile-High Mint, isn't too far from here. Maybe we should try to talk to him?"

"He's got a regular store?" Kyle asks.

"I don't think so, but I have his address from that coin shop cowboy. Maybe he'd talk to us if we just went and asked."

"I want some food!" Annie insists.

"Okay, okay," Kyle says. "Let's get Miss Bottomless Pit some food, and then go find Dan."

We ride the bus to a part of downtown called Larimer Square. All of Denver seems kind of run-down, but this part is different—and less depressing—than out on East Colfax. Instead of bars and pawn shops, this section has neat-looking, older brick and stone buildings with health food stores, restaurants, record stores, and "head shops" that sell psychedelic posters, incense, and leather sandals. Not surprisingly, hippies and other young people swarm the area, and for the first time since we got to Denver, I feel less conspicuous.

We stop to buy tacos from a hole-in-the-wall restaurant, eat them on a nearby bench, and then continue north and east on foot.

We enter an area of old warehouses, factories, office buildings, and hotels. A lot of them have "For Lease" or "For Sale" signs on them, and I note more than a couple of homeless people shuffling around. I hear the whistle of a train not too far away, and remember from the map that we're close to Union Station and Denver's freight yards.

Finally, I find the right street address—a narrow, three-story brick building that looks like it used to be a warehouse of some kind. A few of the ground-floor windows have bars over them, while others have been bricked in altogether. We don't see a sign for the Mile-High Mint— or anything else—on the building. However, a locked, solid metal door has been installed over the regular door, and I spot a tiny doorbell on the wall next to it. I push it.

"I don' hear nothin'," Kyle says after a few seconds.

I push the button again. "Me, either."

"C'mon, let's split," Annie says.

"Would you get the ants outta your pants?" Kyle tells her.

"Kyle, there ain't no one here!"

But just then, a little square window opens in the metal door. I can make out the dim features of a man's nose and eyes.

"Can I help you?"

"Oh," I say, surprised. "We were looking for, uh, Dan Carroll. Is that you?"

"Who wants to know?" The man's voice isn't unfriendly, but it doesn't pulse with warmth, either.

I dig into my pocket for the Love Token and hold it up. "We're, uh, coin collectors, and we found this while we were searching for half dollars."

"Do you want to buy another one? I only accept orders by mail."

"No…sir. A guy at the coin shop on Broadway said you used to work at the U.S. Mint."

"What of it?"

"Well, do you know about the 1964 Peace dollars?"

The man pauses, then answers. "Maybe. Maybe not."

"You see, sir," Kyle steps in. "We know there ain't supposed to be no more and all, but we kinda want to see if we can find one anyway. It's kind of a treasure hunt for us, but it's hard to get any information on 'em."

The metal window closes, and I think, *Well, so much for that idea.*

Kyle, Annie, and I start to turn away, and I begin wondering if I should just go buy my bus ticket back to Florida.

Then, we hear a lock turn behind us, and spin around to see a man standing in the doorway. He's wearing faded jeans, and a tie-dye concert T-shirt for Crosby, Stills, Nash, and Young. He's also wearing cowboy boots and a real Smith & Wesson revolver in a holster on his belt.

He glances warily up and down the street, then studies us closely.

"You don't have any guns or knives on you, do you?"

"No, sir," Kyle answers.

"Good. Come in."

Annie and I glance at each other, but Kyle steps forward, and we follow.

None of us are prepared for what we find inside.

TWENTY-EIGHT

"Wow!" I exclaim, looking around the huge brick-walled room. "This is all yours?"

Lining the walls are workbenches and desks, drawing tables and heavy metal shelves stacked with tools and stuff. *Coin stuff.*

Dan Carroll releases a tiny grin. "Yep. This is where I work."

Even Annie is impressed. "Did you make this?" she asks, walking over to a round plaster cast about two feet in diameter.

"Please don't touch it."

Kyle and I also walk over to look at it. The big round cast holds a jumbo-size design for a new coin or medallion. The image is only partly finished, but shows an upside-down American flag. On one side of the flag is the face of ex-President Nixon with the word "Watergate" under him. The other side features the late President Dwight D. Eisenhower with the phrase "Military Industrial Complex". Around the rim are the words "Rebellion to Tyrants is Obedience to Justice."

"Is this your next project?" I ask, fascinated.

"With all the Bicentennial coins being released," Dan says, "I thought I'd make my own tribute to Liberty and Justice."

"Guess you weren't a big fan of Ike and Tricky Dick," Kyle says.

Dan snorts. "Man, those two did more to destroy this country than anyone."

"Didn't Eisenhower win World War II?" I ask.

"Our *soldiers* won it," Dan says. "When he became president, Ike handed over our economy to the military and weapons manufacturers and put them in charge of government. And Nixon? Well, Watergate wasn't the half of it."

I only understand a little of what he's talking about, but I'm more interested in how he's making the coin. "So what do you do?" I ask. "How do you make this into a coin?"

"Well," he says, warming to us. "I'll show you."

For the next five minutes, he walks us through how he first sketches out his coin designs on paper, and then carves them into plaster. "I send this giant plaster disk to a company in Utah that has special machines that reduce the size of the design and mill it into a master hub."

He holds up a small cylinder of solid steel with the design of a coin on it.

"From this hub," he explains, "we cut the working dies—the ones that actually strike the design into the metal blanks."

"The design is backwards," Annie observes.

"That's right. But when it stamps onto a coin blank, the finished design looks correct."

"And how do you actually, you know, make the coins?" I ask.

"Ah," Dan says, unable to keep the pride off of his face. "That happens over here."

Dominating the back third of the large room is an enormous green machine with electronic control panels next to it.

"Hey, that's just like them machines we saw at the Mint," Annie says.

"That, it is," Dan says. "In fact, this machine came from the Mint. They replaced it with a newer model and auctioned it off. Some of the wiring was bad, and a couple of parts were broken, but I fixed it up to use for my own coins."

"So," I say, "You actually mint your own coins on a machine that used to make *real* U.S. coins?"

Dan grins. "Pretty cool, huh?"

"Yeah," Kyle agrees. "How much did it cost? That machine?"

"Man, it cost more to move it here than it did to buy. The thing weighs about eight tons, and needed an extra-heavy cement pad to set it down on. Fortunately, I found this old factory space here where I could set up shop."

Kyle whistles, and we all stand there admiring the coin press for a few moments.

"But," Dan says. "That's not why you came to see me, is it?"

"No, sir," Kyle says.

"Right," I agree, taking my cue. "Like we said, we're trying to learn more about the 1964 Peace dollars. Everyone's telling us they don't exist, or that if they do, they're already in the hands of some rich collectors, but we thought we'd at least try to find out more about them."

Dan looks at each of our faces, "You Peace dollar collectors?"

"Uh, no," I sheepishly admit. "Nickels, pennies, and quarters mostly."

"And half dollars," Annie joins in.

"Right. And half dollars."

"But we're interested in anything unusual, too," Kyle says. "Y'know, coins that ain't supposed to exist."

"Or are rare or one of a kind," I add.

Dan rests an elbow on the giant coin press. "I can dig it. And what makes you think I know anything about the Peace dollars?"

"Well, like I said, that guy at the coin shop said you worked at the Mint. We thought that maybe you were there when they minted and melted down the Peace dollars."

Dan stays quiet for a moment, staring up at the old-fashioned windows mounted high on the walls of the factory room. Finally, he lowers his eyes and asks, "You're just collectors?"

"Yes, sir," Kyle answers.

"You don't work for anyone else? Treasury? F.B.I.?"

Annie lets out a laugh.

"No," I assure Dan. "We're just doing this on our own."

Dan nods. "Okay, let's sit down."

TWENTY-NINE

D an clears away some old dies and sketches from a workbench in the middle of the room.

"Find some chairs," he tells us. "You want something to drink?"

"No, thank you," Kyle and I tell him.

"You got a Coke?" Annie asks.

Kyle rolls his eyes at her, but Dan nods to a refrigerator. "Right over there. Help yourself."

"I guess I'll have one, too," Kyle calls after her.

"Me, too," I say.

She glances back at us with a smirk.

Dan pulls up his own chair. Before sitting down, he removes the gun from his hip and places it on the table. "Don't worry," he says. "I'm not a gun freak or anything. I got held up once leaving the building. People know I've got valuable stuff in here, so I have to take extra care to protect myself."

I take a closer look at an open cabinet nearby and see stacks of what look like silver coin rounds sitting there, along with some finished coins in plastic tubes.

Annie brings back three Cokes, and hands one to Kyle and me. I pop open my can and take a slurp. "So," I ask, "were you at the Mint during the 1964 Peace dollars' production?"

Dan nods. "I was there alright. Worked through the whole operation. But you know, it wasn't actually in 1964."

"'65, right?" Kyle says.

"That's right. We'd been hearing rumors that we

might make some silver dollars, but we never expected to actually do it."

"Why not?" Kyle asks.

Dan chuckles. "Man, it just didn't make sense. They were already removing precious metals from regular coins, and people were hoarding the older silver coins like crazy. None of us had any doubt that if we made new silver dollars, they'd get snapped up in a flash."

"So why'd they do it?"

"It was all politics. Some senators from somewhere—"

"Montana," I cut in.

Dan nods. "That's right. Montana. They had these romantic notions about silver dollars and talked LBJ—"

"LBJ?" Annie asks.

"President Lyndon Johnson. They talked him into doing it. We just couldn't believe it when the order came down to crank up the presses."

"So what happened?" I ask.

"Well, they decided not to mint the silver dollars in the main Mint building. Because of the national coin shortage, the Mint was short on space, so they had converted the smaller tramway power station into an extra press room. Did you walk behind the Mint building?"

"Shoot," I tell him. "We didn't think of it."

Dan waves his hand. "No sweat, but if you have time, the power station building's still there. We called it the Barn. Anyway, the Mint filled this old power station with about sixteen presses used for making ammunition during World War II. The Mint got the presses from the Department of Defense, and our machinists modified them so they could be used to make coins.

"For making the Peace dollars," Dan continues, "they

modified this enormous Bliss press. Man, that thing was a monster. It could generate 250 *tons* of pressure and could strike two coins at once. Meanwhile, our melting and refining departments were busy making millions of silver blanks that would be fed into the Bliss machine to make the silver dollars."

"Did you say *millions*?" I ask.

"That's right. They prepared more than three million silver dollar blanks for the initial runs."

"But I thought only about three hundred thousand silver dollars were made?"

Dan again waves his hand. "I think it was closer to four hundred thousand but anyway, it took the mechanics a few days to set up that Bliss press so it could handle the silver dollars. When we finally got the go-ahead, it worked like a charm. I was one of the press operators, and it was my job to oil and hand-feed the cartwheel blanks into the feeder tubes, where these little steel tabs called "fingers" automatically picked them up and placed them into the collars to be minted. In no time, we were cranking out brand-new silver dollars like crazy. Soon, they set up a second machine and had it minting Peace dollars, too. This project was ultra-high priority because we had to get them all minted before June 30th, the end of the fiscal year."

"So why'd they stop?" Kyle asks.

Dan again snorts. "Once more, politics! Someone finally came to his senses and realized what a stupid thing it would be to dump all these silver dollars out onto the streets. I mean, you and me would've liked it because we dig coins, but they all would have been gone in a matter of weeks. Congress was already mad at coin collectors, blaming them for the national coin shortage, and they weren't about to give us even more coins to hoard. So, the order came down and we shut down the presses."

"Wow," I say, taking another sip of Coke. "So what happened next? All of the coins were melted?"

Dan nods. "Yep. In fact, the reaction against the silver dollars was so intense that the Treasury and Mint did everything they could to cover it up. They released statements saying they had decided against minting new silver dollars—when they already had hundreds of thousands of them finished and waiting to go out!"

Dan's face is flushed with excitement now. "It was a classic government snafu and everyone was running around trying to cover their backsides. All of us workers at the Mint were under strict orders not to say anything to anyone about it. Later, we had to sign statements that none of us had any of the dollars in our possession, and that all the ones we'd seen had been destroyed. In fact, I could probably get in trouble just for talking to you now."

"But you don't work at the Mint anymore."

"Try telling that to the Treasury Department!"

"So why are you talkin' to us?" Kyle asks.

Dan stares at him, and then at me. Finally, he says, "Well, I just don't see why it *should* be a secret. Who owns the Mint, anyway? Who owns the government? We do! All this Big Brother secrecy stuff is a load 'a crap!"

"So you watched 'em melt down, what, four hundred thousand Peace dollars?" I ask, to get Dan back on track.

He takes a deep breath to calm down. "I didn't actually see it myself, but I had buddies working in the melting and refining departments, and they told me they melted them all, except for some test pieces that had been made earlier at the Philadelphia Mint. They apparently destroyed those a few years later—1970, I think."

"Couldn't some still have survived?" Kyle asks.

"They had very strict procedures for remelting damaged or unwanted coins," Dan says, "and the Mint Police made sure everything went by the book."

"But with three—or four—hundred thousand pieces," I say, "couldn't there have been *some* that got out?"

Dan adopts a formal tone. "As an official ex-Mint employee, I probably shouldn't comment on that."

The way Dan says this gives me the distinct feeling he isn't telling us everything. I decide to press a little harder.

"What about as an *un*official ex-Mint employee?" I ask.

Dan reaches for a nearby copper blank and sets it up on its edge. With a flick of his finger, he sets it twirling rapidly on the table.

Kyle and I glance at each other. No one says anything for a moment. We just watch the copper disk spin. When the disk finally wobbles and clatters back onto the table surface, Dan speaks.

"I'm going to tell you something just between us, okay?"

"Okay," all three of us answer together.

Dan takes a deep breath. "I really shouldn't be repeating this story, but it's something I've thought about almost every day since I worked at the Mint."

"What is it?" I ask.

Dan takes another breath. "Well, while we were working on the Peace dollars, there was a tragic accident."

Kyle and I look at each other, eyes wide. I am imagining a man getting his arm mangled in one of the giant coin presses, so what Dan says next surprises me.

"One night, a friend of mine—another press operator—finished up his shift. He left the Mint building and was crossing Colfax Avenue, when…"

Dan continues staring down at the copper disk on the table.

"When what?" I ask.

"When he got hit by a city bus."

"*What?*" Annie says.

"Yeah, I know," Dan says. "It knocked his body forty feet through the air. He was dead before he hit the ground."

"Geez," I mumble.

Dan looks up from the table. "But that's not why I'm telling you this. The thing is—and I haven't told anyone else this before. The thing is, the police found one of the 1964 Peace dollars in my friend's pocket."

"You're kiddin'!" Kyle exclaims.

Dan shakes his head. "Nope."

"You mean he was tryin' to steal it?" Annie asks.

"He *did* steal it. And he would have gotten away with it, too."

"So what happened?" I ask.

"Well, naturally, they returned the coin to the Mint, but after that, they tightened up security procedures, made us go through metal detectors when we were leaving the Mint."

"So you're sayin'," Annie says, "it's possible other guys was doin' the same thing?"

Dan shrugs. "I'd be lying if I told you otherwise."

"But," I ask, "didn't you say the Mint was also counting all of the silver dollars?"

Dan pauses to consider the question. "Well, not exactly. The Mint didn't actually count the coins when they

melted them. They measured the coins by weight. Someone could have easily replaced one of the '64 dollars with
a silver blank—or an older silver dollar. I'm pretty sure
that's what my friend did—the one who got hit by the bus.
Others could have done the same thing.

"In fact," Dan continues, "another Mint co-worker of
mine told me that he also had one of the Peace dollars, and
had shown it to his friends."

"Crazy," Kyle murmurs.

Dan nods. "That's what he said. The guy was kind of
a blow-hard, though, so take it with a grain of salt. Also,
it's not just us workers who might have taken one. I never did trust all those Treasury and Mint muckety-mucks.
Man, if I were one of them, I would have made *sure* I got
ahold of one of those Peace dollars, wouldn't you?"

"Heck yeah," Kyle says.

"But," I cut in, "that doesn't help us very much. If
someone else got one, there's no way they're going to give
it to us, is there?"

Dan turns both palms upward. "I hate to be the bearer
of bad news, but I doubt it. Still," he says, "it's a fun thing
to think about. I trip about it myself sometimes. It's probably one reason I like minting my own coins and medals.
Holding something that's not only beautiful, but *rare*, in
your hands, well, it's *cool!*"

THIRTY

We gulp down the last of our Cokes and stand up from the workbench.

"Well," I say. "We really appreciate your time."

Dan shrugs. "Hey, it was fun. What's better than sittin' around shootin' the bull about coins, huh?"

Kyle and I laugh.

"In fact, you want to do something fun before you leave?"

The three of us look at each other, and Annie shrugs. "Sure."

"Follow me."

We walk with Dan back to his giant coin press. "I was just about to try stamping out my newest coin. How would you all like to press the buttons?"

I grin. "Yeah!"

"We'll do these in copper," Dan says. From a table next to the press, he carefully picks up a round copper blank that's about the size of a silver dollar, and places it in a collar on the base of the machine.

"See? I've got the reverse die for the coin mounted underneath on what we call the 'stake block'. The obverse die is mounted up above on the 'ram'. This is the part of the machine that actually moves. Here, put on those headphones. It's going to get pretty loud in here."

We each put on a pair of ear protection devices while Dan hits some buttons to start up the machine. Even with the headphones on, loud whirring and clanking reverberates through our bodies.

"This kind of machine is called a knuckle-joint press!" Dan shouts. "It's got a giant flywheel spinning at high speeds, and the flywheel engages with the actual joint to push down the obverse die at massive-crazy pressures!"

Dan does some final checking on the die and copper blank positions and then motions for Annie to step up to the control panel.

"To make it go, it takes both of us pressing down buttons at the same time! Safety device—kinda like those guys in the missile silos who are waiting to fire our nuclear warheads at the Soviet Union! When I press down this black button, you press the red one, okay?"

Even though Annie isn't within three time zones of being a coin collector, she beams. Dan presses down his button and shouts "Bombs away!"

Annie hits her button, and we watch as the joint engages and the obverse die comes down.

THUNK! THUNK!

The whole room shudders as the press stamps the copper blank twice in quick succession.

"I strike my coins twice to give them a nicer finish and more detail," Dan yells over the roar of the machine, "but the Peace dollars were all single-struck."

He uses a giant pair of tongs to remove the finished product. He quickly studies both sides and hands it to Annie. While Dan places another copper blank in the press, Kyle and I crowd in next to Annie to look at her coin.

I expect to see another political coin, but the design surprises me. One side shows a beautiful Egyptian goddess-like figure, while the other side features a pyramid framed by palm trees. Before I can ask about it, Dan asks, "Who's next?"

Kyle shoves me forward and I "mint" my own coin. After Kyle does his, Dan shuts down the machine and we all remove our ear protection.

"Wow, these are beautiful," I tell Dan.

"Yeah, thanks!" Annie gushes.

"Here, let me get you some sleeves to protect them."

Dan walks over to a supply cabinet and returns with some little coin holders like they have in the coin shops. He seals our coins inside and hands them back to us.

"Would you sign the holders for us?" I ask.

Dan shrugs. "Sure, man."

After he signs the coin holders, we thank him again as he straps his gun belt back around his waist. Then, he walks us to the door.

"This has been a big help," I tell him.

"Sure has," Kyle agrees.

"Sorry I didn't have better news for you, but I'll tell you, if I were your age and into coins, I'd be doing the exact same thing. It almost doesn't matter if you find anything. Half the fun is looking."

Well, not quite half, I think.

As he opens the inner door to his shop, though, I suddenly remember what I saw at the Mint.

"Mr. Carroll," I say, "can I ask you one more thing?"

His hand pauses on the door. "Fire away."

"When you worked at the Mint, did you ever see coins flip out of the coin presses by accident, and you know, fall down into the machines?"

Dan takes his hand off the door and adjusts his holster. "Oh yeah, happened all the time. In fact, it's funny you should ask that. When I got this machine, I found more than two hundred coin blanks, finished coins, and mis-struck coins wedged down into the different compartments. No one had ever bothered to tear down the machine and look before they sold it."

"Really?" I pause and ask, "Well, do you know what happened to the two coin presses they used for the silver dollars? I mean, you said you bought yours from a Mint auction. Do you think they're still using the—what did you call them—Bliss presses?"

Dan grins and says, "Ah, I see where you dudes are going with this. It's a good thought, too. But no, I don't have any idea what happened to the presses. I will tell you that while I was helping to mint the silver dollars, I didn't see any coins flip out and slide down into any cracks or anything. That doesn't mean it didn't happen, only that I didn't see it."

Kyle quickly picks up on what I'm thinking. "Do you know how we might find out if those machines are still bein' used?"

"Well, you could ask the Mint office, but I doubt they'd be able to tell you. There's probably records of it somewhere, but that doesn't mean they know how to find them. Tell you what I'll do," Dan says. "I still have friends over there. I'll make a few calls and get back to you."

"You would?" I ask.

"Man, why not? I'd love to see one of those Peace dollars again myself. Where you guys staying?"

"Uh—" I exchange glances with Kyle.

Dan is no dummy. He says, "Hey man, I'm not going to rat you out. I just need a way to get ahold of you."

Kyle nods at me and says, "We're stayin' at the Cottonwood over on East Colfax."

"Gotcha," Dan says. "I'll see what I can find out and

get back to you tomorrow at the latest."

"Sounds good," I tell him.

"Yeah, thanks," Kyle says.

From Dan's workshop, we start walking back toward Larimer Square.

"He sure was nice," I say. "He spent, what, two hours with us?"

Kyle runs his hand through his hair and laughs. "You hard-core coin nerds really love your coins!"

"What're we gonna do now?" Annie asks.

"Not much we can do," Kyle says. "Just go back to the motel and wait."

By now all of us are hungry again, so we grab slices of pizza from a place near Larimer Square. We catch a bus down to Colfax, and another one east to our motel. As the bus rumbles along, I realize I'm feeling sleepy from the morning and eating lunch. I'm looking forward to lying down, even though it means risking a few more bedbug bites. Kyle and Annie also look like they're about to crash.

We pull the cable above the bus window to let us out a few blocks before our motel. As we walk the last couple of blocks, I can already feel the warm bed and the pillow beneath my head. When we're half a block from the motel, however, Annie suddenly clutches my arm and points.

"Look!" she gasps.

THIRTY-ONE

U p ahead, in the parking lot of the Cottonwood, sit two police cruisers with lights silently flashing. Even from where we're standing, it looks like they're parked in front of our room.

"Quick, this way!" Kyle tells us.

We scurry back to the nearest corner and cut left, away from Colfax and into a neighborhood. As soon as we're out of sight of the motel, we start running as fast as we can. Kyle leads us two blocks straight ahead, then turns right, and cuts left again into an alley. I feel more winded than I should—probably because of the altitude here in Denver—but manage to keep up. Annie, though, finally seizes Kyle's arm and hollers, "Y'all wait! I can't run that fast!"

Kyle and I stop to let her catch her breath, then continue at a brisk walk.

"You think they were after us?" I ask Kyle.

"Does a dog howl at the moon?"

"Crap."

"Crap is right. Danny Boy musta called the cops soon as we left."

Annie gives me a shove. "That was your idea to go there, Mike. We shouldn't 'a listened to you."

We exit the alley and, after carefully checking in both directions, cross into the next alley.

"Wait a minute," I say. "You both think Dan Carroll called the police?"

Kyle looks at me. "You got any other explanations?"

"Yeah. Plenty. They could have tracked us down all kinds of ways. That cowboy at the coin shop could have heard about us and called the cops. I saw security cameras at the Mint. Maybe someone recognized us from those."

"Then how'd they find the motel?"

"How hard could it be? They know we don't have much money. All they'd have to do is call the motels all along the strip. Even though we tried to stay hidden, I'm sure the motel manager saw all three of us at one time or another. Shoot, maybe he even called the police himself!"

Kyle and Annie mull this over as we hurry past yards, carports, and trash bins that line the alley. I add, "I just don't think Dan would turn us in like that. He doesn't seem like he'd be the biggest fan of the police or any other authority figures."

Kyle scratches his cheek and finally looks like he's starting to believe me. "Well, it don't matter how they found us. We just gotta think about our next move."

"How're we gonna get our stuff back?" Annie asks.

"We're not," Kyle answers. "We gotta leave it. Anyone leave any money back in the motel?"

Over the last few days, our money has been split up as we've paid for different things, and I stop to reach into my pockets. Annie and Kyle do the same.

"I've got thirty-seven bucks," I say. "I'm pretty sure I didn't leave anything in the motel."

"I've got three hundred and twenty-two," Annie tells us.

"Forty-one," Kyle says.

"That's four hundred bucks," Annie says. "That's gotta be most of what we had left."

"Well, thank god for that. What about other stuff?"

Kyle asks. "Did y'all leave anything that identifies you?"

"Just my clothes," Annie says.

I shake my head. "No. I don't think so. I just had my clothes and—oh, no!"

Kyle looks at me. "What?"

I close my eyes and reopen them. "The *Coin Universe*."

"What about it? Them things are everywhere."

"No, I had a subscription. My address was on it."

"Which address?" Kyle asks. "Florida or California?"

"California."

"Dang."

Up until now, one thing we've had going for us is nobody knew who I was. They had Kyle's and Annie's names, but not mine. That not only made it easier for us to do things, but also kept my parents out of the picture. Now, I can kiss that advantage goodbye.

"I'd better call my dad right away."

"Not your mom?" Kyle asks.

"My dad will be easier to explain it to."

"He's still gonna pitch a fit," Annie tells me.

"Thanks. That's really what I needed to hear."

"First, we gotta find us somewhere else safe," Kyle tells us.

He leads us three more blocks down an alley that seems more run-down and deserted than the others. Near the end sits an old garage in back of a house. Both the garage and the house look like they've seen better days. The garage roof sags and the house looks like it has some kind of skin disease from all the paint peeling off of it.

Kyle stops in front of the garage door, and carefully looks around. Then, he pulls up on the squeaky plywood door to reveal the Bel Air. He quickly waves us inside and brings the door down after us.

"How'd you find this place?" I ask, my eyes adjusting to the dark interior of the structure. The building is an old one, with rough-cut, exposed framing, and a single small, crooked window letting in a cupful of light.

"That's part 'a what I was doin' yesterday when I went out," Kyle explains. "I didn't like the Bel Air sittin' on the street, so I walked around lookin' for 'For Sale' signs. This place didn't look like it'd been lived in for a while, so I figured we might as well chance it."

I nod, studying the bare plank shelves around me. Three Sherwin Williams paint cans with dried, dripping paint down the sides sit on one of the shelves. On another are four unopened cans of Marathon brand motor oil, all covered by a quarter inch of dust. On the cracked cement floor sit a couple of cardboard boxes and a rusted push lawnmower, while on the beams above, I see a few lengths of pipe and what looks like a rats' nest of some sort. I shudder looking at it. Rats are *not* my favorite animals in the world, but fortunately, its residents remain out of sight—for the moment.

"Good hiding place," I tell Kyle.

"It's creepy," Annie says. "I don' wanna stay here."

"We won't. Only 'til we figure what to do next."

"It's too risky to check into another motel," I say. "Probably too risky driving the Bel Air anywhere right now."

"Well, we ain't gonna get very far walkin'. You got any other ideas?"

Kyle and I lean against the Bel Air while Annie explores the rest of the garage. Finally, I tell them, "I hate to say it, but I think yours and Annie's best bet is to leave the Bel Air here, take the money, and hop on a bus north."

Kyle shakes his head, more to himself than to me. "We only got four hundred bucks."

"It's enough to get you to Canada, and like you said, you could probably get a job pretty easily up there."

"I want to go to California," Annie says. "We can live by the beach. I can learn to surf."

Kyle doesn't even respond to that. "It's just that I don't see how we'd be that much better off in Canada," he tells me.

"Well, you won't be in jail for one thing. That's pretty big."

"Yeah. But what about that silver dollar? Seems like we're gettin' closer."

"Maybe, but do you think we should keep looking with the cops swarming all over the place? Assuming Dan Carroll didn't turn us in, he's going to call the motel with information and we won't be there."

"We could go back and see him."

"Today? Are you crazy?"

"No, maybe early in the mornin'," Kyle says.

"All three of us together? We'd be picked up in a flash."

"Well, then *you* could go and see him by yourself. Even if they track down your mom, they still ain't gonna have a picture of you by then."

"What are we going to do in the meantime?"

Kyle looks all around the garage. "Well, at least there aren't bedbugs here."

"I'm not sleepin' here in this garage!" Annie protests.

"We'll round up some blankets and sleep in the car,"

Kyle tells her. "It won't be so bad."

"I wish I'd stayed in Alabama."

Silence descends on the garage, and Kyle and I look at each other. Even as self-centered as Annie can be, what she just said is, well, shocking.

She'd rather stay in Birmingham with her abusive uncle than be here with us?

Kyle also looks confused, but neither of us can think of a response. Annie turns her back to us, and I mutter, "I'd better go find a pay phone."

THIRTY-TWO

I am hoping to reach my dad before he gets a call from the police or my mom.

Too late.

By the time I reach a payphone on Colfax and make the call, my dad can barely control himself.

"Mike, what do you think you're doing?" he shouts into the phone. "I was just getting ready to fly out to Denver to try to find you! Your mom phoned me an hour ago almost hysterical. She got a call from the Denver Police Department saying you were on the run with Kyle and his sister. Is that true?"

"No. Yes. Let me explain."

"You'd better and you'd better do it *fast!*"

As best as I can, I try to tell my dad how I ended up with Kyle and Annie in Colorado. To his credit, he lets me talk without interrupting me. I tell him how I didn't know what Kyle's plan was, but when I learned about Annie and her uncle, I thought I could help. When I finish telling my story, I close my mouth and wait for my father's angry response.

Instead, I hear him take a deep breath on the other end of the connection.

"Look, son. I think I understand why you're doing this, but the bottom line is that this isn't your battle. Kyle and Annie are in a tough situation, but they've made it worse by how they're dealing with it. They shouldn't be dragging you into it with them."

"They're not dragging me—"

"I'm not finished," my dad tells me. "Mike, I know you think you're doing the right thing and, honestly, you're almost old enough to make your own decisions. But the key word is *almost*. Even though we're divorced, your mother and I are still responsible for you. And I'm telling you, you need to get back here *now!*"

"Dad, I—"

"I'm going to book an airplane ticket for you from Stapleton Airport for tomorrow morning. Can you get there okay?"

"Yeah, but—"

"No buts, Mike. Do you have a place to stay? Do you have enough money for a motel room?"

"Yes, but what about Kyle and Annie?"

I hear another sigh on the other end. Then, my dad says, "They've got to make their own decisions, but if you're a real friend, you should advise them to turn themselves in. The police are really after them now. Maybe even the F.B.I."

"*The F.B.I.?*"

"This is no game, son. You've crossed state lines and abducted a minor—at least that's how law enforcement is going to see it. Other people are looking for you, too."

"Who?"

"Kyle and Annie's uncle tracked me down to see if I knew anything. I told him I thought you were in Denver, but he already knew that. He's going out there to try to find them. Find *you*."

My chest tightens. "*He is?*"

"He might already be there."

"You didn't tell him anything else, did you?"

"Mike, I didn't *know* anything else!"

"But he might come after Annie. Try to hurt her or shut her up."

The operator comes on, asking me to put more change into the pay phone, but my dad tells her to reverse the charges.

Then, my dad says, "If they're really worried about that, they should just go to the police and tell them everything. The longer they run, the worse it's going to get for them."

I don't say anything.

"Mike, you still there?"

"Yes."

"Get to the airport by seven o'clock tomorrow morning and go to the Eastern Airlines counter. Your ticket will be waiting for you. Do you understand?"

"Yes."

"Good. Be careful son. I love you."

I hang up the phone feeling like I've just been thrown in a blender. I realize, though, that all in all, my dad let me off pretty easy.

Glancing around, I carefully open the phone booth door, and then hurry down a side street back toward the garage where the Bel Air is stashed. Walking back, I replay the phone conversation between my dad and me, looking for some loophole, or at least some wiggle room.

There isn't any.

Mike, you're just going to have to make a decision. Are you going to stay and disobey your parents and make them frantic with worry, or are you going to abandon your friends and slink away with your tail between your legs?

As I cross a street, I catch a view of the mountains to the west. The sun has set, but bright orange clouds still slash the evening sky. I stop for a moment to look at them. I've got twelve hours before my plane takes off.

Twelve hours to make my decision.

It takes me two tries to retrace my steps back to the garage, but I finally find it. I jump a little fence so that I can go in through the door on the "house side" of the garage, and tap lightly before I go in. With the fading light, it's even darker inside than it was before, but I make out the dim figures of Kyle and Annie both sitting in the front seat of the Bel Air, doors open. Seeing me, Kyle climbs out and leans his arms on the car's roof.

"How'd it go?"

I walk around to his side. "Not so good. The police had already called my mom and my dad heard about us from her."

"That's a drag," Kyle says and, as if it's a reminder, he reaches in his pocket for his cigarettes. As he's lighting up, I glance into the car's interior and see Annie busily munching on a bag of Fritos. She doesn't make eye contact with me, and I can tell she's royally pissed about something—probably a lot of things.

"You got some food," I say. "I should have thought of that."

"Yeah. Found a 7-Eleven not too far from here. Jimmied my way into the house here, too, and found a few blankets."

"They got rat holes in 'em," Annie finally says from inside the car.

"They'll keep us warm," Kyle shoots back, but the word "rats" makes my own skin crawl as well.

"So what'd your dad say?" Kyle asks.

I hesitate, debating if I should tell them about their uncle coming out to Denver. If Kyle and I were alone, I'd just tell him, but I don't want Annie to freak out. At least not right now.

Besides, I reason. *What are the chances their uncle can find us in this huge city?*

Instead of telling them about their uncle, I say, "My dad wants me to come home."

"You going to?"

I shrug. "I haven't made up my mind. He also said I should try to talk you into turning yourselves in. He said it's just going to get tougher for you the longer you run."

"I'm not goin' to jail," Annie says.

Kyle takes a hit on his cigarette. "Maybe your dad's right. What would you do, Mike?"

I lean back against the Bel Air, and honestly answer, "I don't know. Maybe we need to sleep on it."

"I don't wanna sleep in this car, neither," Annie hollers.

"Too bad," Kyle tells her, "because that's exactly what we're gonna do."

Even with the knowledge that rats are around, I sleep better than I expect—for a while, anyway. Annie is too mad at her brother to share a seat with him, so Kyle stretches out in front while Annie and I try to get comfortable on opposite ends of the back bench seat. I fall right to sleep for a couple of hours, but even though the day was warm, the night cools down rapidly at the high altitude. With only one blanket covering me, I wake up shivering, and try to curl tightly into a ball.

Then, I feel Annie's warm body snuggle up to mine.

"I'm cold," she whispers.

Having been a Boy Scout, I am plenty aware of the

concept of sharing body heat, but I hesitate just the same. This is my friend's sister, after all, and she is still three whole years younger than I am. I'm also feeling a little protective of her because of the beatings she received from her uncle. I'm not exactly sure how that relates to the current situation, but am sure that it does somehow.

Still, I reason, *she is making the first move.*

If nothing else, the need for body warmth overcomes all other considerations. I put my arm around her and in a flash, our bodies are pressed tightly against each other—which creates some entirely new sensations and concerns.

Even though I am sixteen years old, I have never been this, well, *intimate* with a girl before. Sure, I was boyfriend/girlfriend with Sharon Lundgard for a few weeks, and we shared one awkward—and totally lame—kiss. Other than that, I'm pretty sure I'm the only sixteen year-old who has been totally left behind by the Era of Free Love.

That's not to say that girls don't interest me. They do, and in a major way. It's just that women—girls—haven't exactly flocked to take advantage of my dashing looks, wit, and other charms.

Annie and I lie curled together for a few moments, and I stop shivering. I can feel her warm breath on my neck every time she exhales, and my heart refuses to dip down out of the red zone. I try to stay absolutely still, not wanting to break the spell of this pleasant, unanticipated circumstance.

Then, Annie lifts her mouth to my ear and whispers, "Mike, you like me, dontcha?"

I don't answer right away. Instead, I listen closely to try to tell if Kyle is asleep. His steady, slow breath assures me that he is.

"Uh, yeah," I whisper back to Annie.

She squeezes me a little harder. "Thought so. I could tell by the way ya look at me."

She can? It's news to me—and not very comforting to be that obvious.

"I like you, too," she whispers. "You're not like most 'a the guys I know."

"I'm not?"

"You're nicer. Most guys, they're just tryin' to score, get somethin' so they can brag to their friends about it. You're not like that."

"Oh…"

Then, Annie does something that surprises me even more. She lifts her head up off of my shoulder and presses her lips quickly against mine. Her lips are a little chapped, and her mouth tastes faintly of Fritos, but I don't spend too long thinking about that. What I'm focusing on is the shuddering waves of delight passing from my lips down to every cell of my body.

After a few seconds, Annie pauses and whispers, "You ain't kissed many girls, have ya?"

I pull away, embarrassed. "Uh, Annie, I don't think we should be talking about this."

"Why not?"

That's the question. *Why not?* But all I can say is, "Uh, I just don't think we should."

Annie smiles and kisses me again.

"You're sweet," she says.

Then, she closes her eyes and goes back to sleep.

▼

THIRTY-THREE

Annie's two kisses pretty much ensure that I won't fall back to sleep right away—maybe not ever again. My eyes stare up at the roof of the Bel Air, marveling at what just happened. I breathe in the sweet scent of Annie's hair, study her face, and feel her pressed against me under the blankets. I have to admit that I'm a bit confused by it all. Annie is so grown up in some ways, but in a lot of others, she still seems like a little girl.

Should I really be having the feelings for her that I do?

It doesn't matter if I should or shouldn't. I just do. Maybe it's true that girls are more mature than boys. I don't know, but I do know that right at this moment, I wouldn't change a thing.

In the next instant, I feel a hand pushing against my shoulder.

"Mike, wake up!"

I crack my eyes open. The light is still dim inside the garage, but I can tell that the sun has risen outside, and I see Kyle studying me—studying *us*—from the front seat.

"Oh." I quickly extract myself from Annie's grasp and sit up. She rolls away from me with a little grunt, but doesn't fully wake. My eyes swing from her back to Kyle.

"It got cold last night," I mumble weakly.

Kyle continues to stare at me for another moment, and I wonder if he's going to punch me out. Instead, he gives a little shake of his head and says, "Did you decide what you're gonna do?"

I again glance at the light coming through the tiny garage window, and think, *If I hurry, I can probably still get to the airport to catch my plane.*

But that's not what I'm going to do. If I had any doubts about that, the sleeping girl next to me put an end to them last night.

I turn my eyes back to Kyle and say, "I think that you and Annie should get out of town before the cops close in on us. I'll go back to Florida. Before we do that, though, we should try to find a 1964 Peace dollar."

Kyle gives a tight smile. "That's exactly what I was thinkin'."

"We can go back to Dan Carroll's place and ask him what he found out," I say. "If we can track down the coin presses used to make the Peace dollars, we might just have a chance to find one of them hidden inside."

Kyle's smile stretches into a grin. "You read my mind. You think one of us should go alone or all go together?"

"It'd be a lot safer for just me to go," I reason, "but we don't have much time. If we find out anything from Dan—and even if we don't—we're going to have to move fast. Besides, Annie's not going to want to stay behind."

At the mention of Annie's name, an awkward silence falls between us. I study Kyle's expression, trying to read if he's mad at me. He's no dummy. Even though Annie's kisses were pretty innocent, I'm sure he's put two and two together that I might be having some feelings toward her. I wouldn't blame him if he got angry. But it's not anger I see on his face. It's worry. Worry about his sister. Maybe worry about all of us.

"We'll all go together," he decides, and climbs out of the Bel Air.

I scramble out after him. "You think you can avoid the police?"

"Maybe. You see our new license plates?"

"Huh?"

I walk around to the front of the car. Instead of Florida plates, the Bel Air now sports a nice set of red-and-whites from Colorado.

"That's what I was doin' when I went out the other day. That and findin' this hidin' spot."

"Smart."

"Still, ain't that many Bel Airs around. We gotta be careful, and you and Annie gotta keep your heads down."

Kyle calls into the car. "Annie, get up. We gotta go."

She moans and mutters, "Leave me here. I wanna sleep."

Kyle reaches in and yanks on her foot. "Get up. Now."

"Okay. Okay."

I see her head rise up from the back seat and my heart does a little flip. Her blonde hair sticks out in all directions, single strands turned to gold from the light coming through the window. When she sees me, her mouth curves into a big smile.

"How'd ya sleep?" she asks me, but that's not what she's really asking.

I smile back at her. "Pretty well."

"C'mon, we gotta go," Kyle barks.

After we all take turns peeing in the overgrown backyard of the house, Kyle opens the garage door, and we pile into the Bel Air. Kyle turns the ignition and the Bel Air roars.

We prowl through alleys, maintaining a careful lookout for police. Annie keeps her head down in the back, while I slump way down in front.

"See anything?" I ask Kyle as we swing back onto East Colfax.

"Just regular traffic."

"Good."

"Can y'all stop at McDonald's again?" Annie asks.

"Too dangerous," Kyle tells her.

"So's starvin' to death."

A laugh escapes me before I can stifle it.

"Fine," Kyle huffs, and we quickly pull into a drive-through.

After we order, we pull forward and Kyle takes our bag of food and a couple of coffees from the pick-up window. He's just about to pull out when he glances in the rearview mirror.

"Dang it."

I am still slouched down, but lift my head enough to look into the side mirror. Three cars back, just pulling up to the ordering station, is a Denver Police cruiser.

"Do they see us?"

Kyle puts the Bel Air into first gear and eases forward. "Don't think so."

"Does who see us?" Annie's lifts her head and looks out the back window.

"Annie, get down!" Kyle hisses.

As we head out of the parking lot, I continue to watch the police car in the sideview mirror. It looks like we're going to slip away unnoticed, but just as we're about to turn left, out of view, I see one of the policemen suddenly look directly toward us. His mouth opens.

"Punch it!" I shout.

With a screech of rubber, Kyle tears out of the parking lot, cutting in front of a line of cars heading west toward downtown. The closest car swerves and honks angrily at us.

"Did the cops see us?" Annie asks, sitting up again.

"Get off of Colfax!" I yell.

I keep looking back, waiting for the police car to come into view. Kyle races to the next street and twists the wheel into a hard right.

"Are they following us?" he asks.

"I can't tell! Don't slow down!"

The Bel Air roars down another block and skids through a left turn, onto an even smaller street.

"See anything?"

"Nothin' behind us," Annie says from the back seat.

"I don't hear any sirens, either," I say.

Kyle eases off the gas. "Good. They probably got trapped in the drive-through."

"You'd better stick to these side streets."

"That's exactly what I'm fixin' to do."

Getting out the map, I navigate while Kyle zigzags north and then west through tree-lined neighborhoods, back toward downtown. At any moment, I'm expecting to hear sirens wail and see flashing lights behind us, but we make it to the warehouse district without further incident.

"It's too risky for us all to go in," Kyle says as we approach Dan Carroll's place. "Mike, I'm gonna drop ya off and then find a safe place to park where I can see the front door. You talk to Danny Boy, see if he knows anythin', then hurry back out."

"What if the cops are waitin' for him?" Annie asks. I note with satisfaction the real worry in her voice.

Maybe she really does like me.

"I don't think Dan would turn us in," Kyle says.

"Right, Mike?"

I shake my head.

"But if somethin' does happen and we have to burn it outta here, you got enough cash for a bus ticket home?"

"Don't worry about me," I tell him. "Just get away, safe."

I again debate whether I should tell him that his uncle is on his way from Alabama, but Annie is still here and before I can make up my mind, Kyle pulls up in front of the Mile-High Mint.

"Good luck," Kyle says.

"Yeah," Annie tells me and reaches over to squeeze my shoulder.

Our eyes meet and my heart again does a little leap.

"Be right back," I tell them both.

THIRTY-FOUR

I scurry out of the Bel Air and up to the front door of Dan's shop. I breathe in the cool morning air, and with it, the stale, beer-scented smell of dirty cement sidewalk. I push the buzzer and then pivot anxiously in a circle. The Bel Air disappears around the corner, and I spot a few other vehicles parked on the street, but traffic always seems light in this part of town. I hear the little window open in the steel door behind me and I whirl toward it. I catch a glimpse of Dan's face, but today there's no hesitation. Locks click and the door bursts open.

Dan is standing there wearing a different tie-dye shirt, but the same gun on his hip. He motions his hand impatiently. "Hurry! Get in here!"

I rush inside and after a quick glance at the street, Dan closes and relocks the doors. Then, he turns toward me. "You cats are in some hot water, aren't you?"

I consider lying, but there doesn't seem any point. "A little."

He walks farther into his workshop, and I follow. "The Man showed up about an hour after you left yesterday."

I stop, alarmed. "You mean the police? They did?"

"No sweat. I didn't tell them anything."

"Do they know we were here?"

"Yeah, but I told them I didn't even let you inside. Just told you to beat it on out of here."

I rub my hand over my face. "Geez. Thanks."

"I think they bought it," Dan continues. "But you

never know. If I were you, I'd get lost for a while. *Really* lost. Anyway, I got some information for you. Over here."

I follow him to a workbench next to a telephone. He tears a piece of paper off of a little white pad. "So, I called one of my buddies at the Mint. He said that, like I told you before, both of those coin presses they used for the Peace dollars were made to make ammunition during World War II. The Mint got them from the Department of Defense, but they replaced them a few years ago."

"What happened to them?"

"Apparently, they were sold to a used equipment dealer here in Denver. My buddy knows the guy who bought them and thinks one of them went overseas, maybe to some little island country that wants to start minting its own coins with the face of their favorite dictator on them."

"What about the other one?"

Dan grins. "That's the good news. The other press was in pretty bad shape. This equipment dealer couldn't sell it to anybody, and finally, a junk man bought it. As far as my friend knows, that press is still sittin' in the scrap yard. I can't guarantee it's still there, but here's the address."

I take the piece of paper from him. "Thanks."

"Man, I hope you find a Peace dollar. That would be outta sight."

Dan walks me back to the door. "You guys keep cool, you hear?"

"We will."

As Dan puts his hand on the door handle, though, I ask him. "Can I ask you why you didn't tell the police about us?" A shadow flits across Dan's face. "Aw, I don't know. You three don't look like criminals. Are you?"

I shake my head. "No."

"That's what I figured. I figure if you're running, there's probably a good reason for it. Thought you deserved a shot."

"But you could have gone after the Peace dollar yourself."

Dan says nothing for a moment, but drops his hand from the door handle. "Hey, I gotta admit, it crossed my mind, but..."

"But what?"

He nods toward the door. "You know that girl that was with you?"

"Annie?"

"Yeah, well, I got a girl—a daughter—a little older than her. Seventee—make that eighteen."

"Here in Denver?"

His eyes stare away from me. "Man, wish I knew. She took off a couple years ago and I haven't seen her. Maybe I just figure if I help you, someone'll help her, you dig?"

"Yeah."

"Yeah. Besides, as a former Mint employee, it wouldn't look good for me to suddenly 'find' one of those coins, now, would it?"

"I guess not." I turn and look Dan straight in the eyes. "Thanks."

Dan's eyes focus back on me. "Don't mention it, but do me a favor, okay?"

"What?"

"Let your parents know where you are."

"Okay."

"And one other thing. You find that Peace dollar, you send me a postcard, okay?"

I smile. "We will."

The moment I step out the door, Kyle spots me and roars up to the curb. I jump into the Bel Air.

"What'd Dan say?" Annie demands, leaning forward from the back seat.

"The police came to visit him yesterday."

Annie's eyes flare. "So Dan *was* the one who turned us in! That snake!"

"Annie, he did *not* turn us in," I tell her. "In fact, he told them he'd run us off and hadn't seen us since."

"What about the coin presses?" Kyle asks, pulling away from the curb.

"Well, that's the real news. One of them got sold overseas, but the other one is in a scrap yard not too far from here."

Kyle slaps his hand on the steering wheel. "Knew it! Which way?"

I find the address on our map and give Kyle directions. From Dan's place, we follow Market Street up to 40th Avenue and head east, paralleling Interstate 70 and the Union Pacific tracks until we see a large pet food factory.

"Phew! That stinks," Annie says from the back seat.

"Not if you're a dog," Kyle tells her.

I snort, but do another quick scan for law enforcement before returning my attention to the map.

"It should be just up here," I tell Kyle.

Past the pet food factory, we take a left. This whole area has an industrial feel to it, with warehouses, abandoned vacant lots, and rail sidings leading into factories surrounded by chain-link fencing.

I point. "There it is."

Up ahead, we see a large painted sign reading "Global Recycling".

Kyle pulls into a parking area of crumbling asphalt. Despite the lofty name, the huge expanse behind the fence looks like every other junk yard I've ever seen.

"Do you want me to go in?" I ask.

"You stay here," Kyle tells us. "No one oughta be expectin' us here, and besides, I got what you'd call experience in places like this."

Kyle gets out of the car, and Annie hops up into the front seat with me. "You want your breakfast now?" she asks.

"Oh, yeah." In all the excitement of the morning, I've totally forgotten about our food, but when the smell of the egg sandwich hits my nose, my stomach rumbles loudly.

"You think he'll find that coin press in there?"

I shrug and in a single bite, tear off a third of the sandwich. "Probably. Dan said it wasn't working, so I don't know why anyone would buy it."

Annie reaches out and slides her fingertips through my hair. "So," she asks me, "do you still like me this morning?"

I almost choke on my sandwich and reach for my cup of coffee. After gulping down a huge swallow, I smile at her, hoping there's no egg in my teeth. "What do you think?"

She leans over and kisses me on the cheek.

I feel my face warm. "But Annie, do you think we should be doing this now?"

A hurt look crosses her face. "Why not?"

"I mean with Kyle here."

"He's *not* here. He's in there," she says, pointing through the fence.

"I know," I fumble. "I mean, I just don't know if he'd

like us doing, you know…"

"Kissin'? That's none 'a his business! We like each other, don't we?"

"Well, yeah."

"Or did ya change your mind?" Annie pulls her hand back into her lap and looks at me as if I just slapped her.

"No!" I blurt. "Of course I like you! I just, uh, well…"

"Cause if you changed your mind, all you got to do is tell me, Mike! I been dumped before and you ain't the only guy in the world—"

"Annie, that's not what I mean. I just mean that Kyle's my friend and—"

"And you're sayin' he's more important to you than I am?"

"No! That's not it!"

I am totally turned around now.

"Annie," I try again. "I like you a lot. I think I like you more than any other girl I've ever spent time with!"

That calms her a bit.

"But with everything that's happening, I don't want you to get hurt. Today—tomorrow at the latest—you and Kyle are going to take off, and I'm going to go back to Florida."

"So?" she insists. "We can still write to each other and visit each other."

"It's not just that. I mean, I'm three years *older* than you are. And besides, there's this whole thing with your uncle."

Her lip juts out stubbornly. "What about my uncle?"

"You know," I tell her. "How he's treated you. How mean he's been, hitting you and everything."

Annie throws up her hands and exclaims, "Mike, you

are so dumb! Don't you get it?"

I look at her, confused. "Get what?"

Annie fixes me with her pale blue eyes, and says, "It's not true."

I'm still not following her. "What's not true?"

"Mike, my uncle never hit me!"

nnie's statement silences me. At first, I think I've misunderstood.

"What?" I finally say.

Annie looks away and starts fiddling with the Bel Air's rectangular window wing.

"I said my uncle never hit me."

"You mean..."

"I made it up so's Kyle would come and get me."

My mind continues to crawl. "Wh-what about that bruise?"

She turns back to me and reaches up to her cheek. "This? Oh, I was playin' football with some girls, and one of 'em drilled the ball straight into my face. Gave me a black eye and a bloody nose."

Now I feel like *I've* been hit.

"But, Annie..."

"I know I prob'ly shouldn't have said it was from my uncle, but I didn't have no choice. I hated it there. I couldn't stand it for another minute."

I drop my sandwich into my lap and fall back against the seat.

"Oh, all that other stuff I told you was true," Annie continues. "Not locking me in the closet, but the other stuff. About how mean he and my aunt were and how they told me I was goin' to hell and everythin'."

"Yeah, but Annie. What you said about your uncle..."

"I know. It wasn't very nice."

"Annie, it was worse than that. You accused him of...

child abuse."

Her face reddens. "I did no such thing!"

"You did, Annie! Don't you see? You say those kinds of things about a person, it can destroy him! It doesn't even have to be true. All it takes is a rumor and that person's reputation is down the tubes—forever!"

"But he *didn't* do it," Annie protests.

"But how are people going to know that? You think they're going to believe him against a pretty thirteen year-old girl who's lost both her parents?"

Annie's face remains stubbornly fixed. "But he was still mean to me."

"That doesn't matter!" I am really getting worked up now. "I mean, it matters, but it's something totally different. What you said was a total lie. It's not just going to hurt your uncle. What about all the kids who really *are* beaten up or abused in other ways? If your lies get out, who is going to believe them now?"

"Well, that's what gave me the idea," Annie explains. "When Kyle and me was in Florida, somethin' like that really happened to a friend of mine. I thought I could use it here to get Kyle to come and get me."

I look into her eyes and can tell she's entirely missing the point.

"Did you tell Kyle the truth?"

"No!" she shouts. "And don't you tell him neither. He'd kill me if he found out."

"You have to tell him, Annie. Kyle wanted to kill your uncle when we got to Birmingham."

Annie waves it off. "Oh, he's always sayin' stuff like that."

I grab her shoulder and shake it. "Annie, no! He

meant it! He really wanted to *kill* him!"

Finally, my words start to sink in. Annie's face sags, and she mutters. "He wouldn't have."

"Annie!" I repeat. "You've got to tell him. You tell him or I will!"

Her eyes widen and she clutches my T-shirt. "Mike, no! You can't! I'll do anything. Just don't tell Kyle. *Please!*"

I rip myself away and hurl myself out of the car. I stomp over to the chain-link fence, curl my fingers through the links, and give it a vicious kick. The percussion of the metal rattles in both directions. My heart and mind are swirling like giant tide pools, sucking me under. This whole adventure—this whole trip—was based on helping out a friend. Now, I find that every bit of it is a lie. I let go of the fence and stalk away from the Bel Air.

The junk yard is probably two hundred yards long and I kick stones as I walk along the street toward the far end. What Annie has told me is so screwed up, I just don't know how to respond. Her life in Birmingham, yeah, it was probably awful. Worse than anything I've had to live through—even my parents' divorce. But telling Kyle and me that her uncle beat her and locked her in the closet...

I think again about Kyle and how he just assumed everything Annie told him was true. He didn't hesitate to go and rescue her.

She took advantage of him. She used him. He trusted her—he still *trusts her. If she won't tell him, should I?*

I hear a horn honk behind me and spin around to see Kyle waving at me to come back to the Bel Air. I hesitate. I don't feel like being anywhere near Annie until I can sort this out. Unfortunately, that's not a luxury I have. I kick one last rock and head back to the car.

I climb into the front passenger seat, but don't look at Annie or Kyle. Kyle is too excited to notice.

"It's there, Mike! The coin press! There were too many people around for me to look through it, but just pokin' around a little, I found this."

He hands me a medium-sized disk. At first I don't see it, my mind still fogged by what Annie's told me.

"What is it, exactly?" Kyle asks me.

"Oh…" I drop my eyes to the disk in my hands and try to shift brain gears. It's not easy. As my eyes focus, however, I see that the object I'm holding is heavily tarnished.

Silver for sure.

My interest sharpens. One side of the disk is blank, but stamped into the other side is the eagle for the reverse design of a quarter, or twenty-five cent piece.

I am astonished. "You found this in the machine?"

Kyle grins. "And I'm sure there's others in there, too. We just need time to look through it—with some tools."

And now I can't help myself. I start to get excited about what Kyle has found, and I have to admit I'm surprised. Even though I'd seen a coin slip into a coin press during our Denver Mint tour, I never really expected to find such a thing ourselves.

"Did you talk to the scrap yard owner?" I ask.

Kyle nods. "Told him I was lookin' for a new muffler. Then, after I found the coin press, I went back and asked him what he was gonna do with it."

"And?"

"He said the thing don't work no more and he'd sell it for parts, but no one's buyin'."

"So he doesn't want it?"

Kyle laughs. "He said he'd almost pay someone to

come haul it away. The thing weighs, like, fifteen tons."

Annie has stayed silent the whole time in the back seat, but again, Kyle is too worked up to notice.

"So what do you want to do?"

"The place closes at five," Kyle says. "I figure we just hide out until it starts to get dark. Then, we come back and do a complete search of the machine."

"How are we going to get in?"

Kyle winks at me. "I got that covered."

THIRTY-SIX

It's still only about noon, so Kyle finds us a convenience store to buy yet another balanced meal of potato chips, soda, and soggy pre-made baloney sandwiches. I'm craving a real meal—even one with vegetables—but it's too risky to go into a restaurant. Besides, in this part of town, we don't have a lot to choose from. The upside is that there don't seem to be a lot of police around, either. We see only one black-and-white cruiser and it pays us no notice. I guess we fit in pretty well out here in the world of junk yards, factories, and warehouses. Or maybe Kyle's new Colorado plates actually help camouflage us.

Groceries in hand, Kyle finds an out-of-the-way spot behind some kind of sheet-metal factory that looks closed. He parks the Bel Air so that we're hidden from the street, and we begin to wait it out through the long afternoon. After stuffing ourselves on empty calories, Kyle goes for a walk to stretch his legs while Annie takes a nap in the back seat—which is fine with me because she and I haven't said two words to each other since our earlier exchange. I am waiting for her to tell Kyle the truth about her uncle, but she hasn't shown any sign of doing it, and I debate how long I should wait before telling Kyle myself—or even if I *should* tell him.

If I do tell him, Annie'll probably never speak to me again. But if I don't tell him, an innocent man could get hurt. Worse than that—ruined.

It's a no-win situation for me, but it's not my only worry. Since skipping my airline flight, my dad must be freaking out. I would be if I were him.

I probably should call him, but I reason that it'll only make matters worse.

One way or another, I tell myself, *this will all be over by tomorrow, and I'll call him then.*

I try not to think about how much trouble I'm in. I should be angry. If Annie had told the truth, none of this ever would have happened. But when I glance back at her asleep in the back seat, it's not anger that I feel. It's a kind of numbness, a determination to just get through the next twenty-four hours one way or the other.

Maybe I'm in denial, I think, but then I recognize it as something else. Something I've actually felt before. It was when my parents were getting divorced and my mom got married to my stepfather, the accountant. Yeah, I remember it now—a simple mindset that if I didn't want to get swallowed and chewed up by what was going on around me, all I could do was take things one moment at a time, hang on by my fingernails, and hope that I'd come out the other side.

Kyle returns after a while and we talk more about the Peace dollar. I'm pretty sure Annie's listening to us from the back seat but is pretending to still be asleep. Then, Kyle decides to work on the Bel Air. He pulls his tools out of the trunk and gets busy adjusting the gaps, checking the timing, and doing other stuff I don't really understand. Sometime during the afternoon, I doze off, scrunched up against the front passenger door. I wake when I hear Annie crawl out the back window to go relieve herself.

I open my eyes and sit up straight. Kyle has obviously finished working on the Bel Air and has his eyes closed behind the steering wheel. He opens them when he hears me stir.

"What time is it?" I ask. I look up at the sky to try to locate the sun, but a dark layer of thunderheads has moved in while I was napping.

Kyle yawns. "Quittin' time—at least for everyone else. Traffic's been pickin' up. People goin' home after work. We can make our move pretty soon."

"There's still a lot of light."

"With these clouds, it'll get dark fast. We might even get rained on."

On cue, I see a flash of lightning off to the north.

"I wish we had raincoats."

Kyle shrugs. "A little water won't hurt us. Might even help cover our tracks."

Annie returns and Kyle hops out to let her into the back. Hopping back in, he spins to look at her. "How ya doin', Sis?"

"Okay," she says, not meeting his eyes. "So what's the plan? After we hit this junk yard, we gonna get outta this state?"

"After we get us that Peace dollar, yep. That's what we're gonna do."

Annie snorts. "Y'all ain't gonna find no silver dollar."

"Yeah? You watch us."

"Whatever," Annie says. "I jes' wanna put Colorado behind me. Way behind me."

Kyle starts up the Bel Air. "Soon as we get rich."

We drive a mile or so back to the scrap yard and slowly cruise by it—what we criminals like to call "casing the joint". It's probably six o'clock by now and the place indeed looks deserted. Thanks to the thunderheads, it feels almost safe to go in.

"You see any dogs?" Kyle asks.

"No, but he's got some floodlights set up."

Kyle cranes his head toward the scrap yard. "Yeah, I spotted those earlier. I don't think they'll bother us none. That coin press is sittin' most of the way to the back. Even under the lights, we'll be too far away for anyone to see us from the street."

"How are we going to get in?" Not only does the chain-link fence surround the scrap yard, ribbons of razor wire lace the top.

"I'll show ya," Kyle says.

He continues past the yard and parks behind some elm trees a quarter mile away.

We get out and he pulls a pair of bolt cutters from the trunk and hands them to me. He also selects two screwdrivers, a flashlight, and an adjustable crescent wrench, placing them all in a greasy, empty pillowcase.

"What're those for?" Annie asks, watching him, a comfortable distance from where I stand.

"In case we want to dig into the guts of that coin press to look around."

"Good thinking," I say.

Kyle closes the trunk and hands Annie the keys. "Okay, Annie. You stay here. We might be awhile, but you see anything happen to us, you take the Bel Air and get as far away from here as you can."

"*Without y'all?*" The reality of what we're doing seems to strike Annie for the first time.

"You'll be okay," Kyle tells her. "Besides, nothin's gonna happen to us. We'll be back in half an hour, an hour tops, okay?"

"Let me come with you," Annie pleads.

Kyle stands firm. "It's too dangerous."

I look at her and think, *Tell him the truth, Annie. Tell him now.*

She just stands there, fear and uncertainty on her face.

THIRTY-SEVEN

K yle leads me to the corner of the scrap yard and shows me how we're going to enter.

"They spent all this money on fencin', and then they just attached the corners with plain 'ole baling wire."

"Looks like the fence broke before and they just patched it up with the wire," I observe.

"Yep."

Of course Kyle is something of an expert at sneaking into places. We never would have found the Confederate double eagles two years ago if he hadn't shown me how to sneak into that Civil War fort in Alabama. Tonight, our task is even easier. After three snips with the bolt cutters, we're able to peel back the chain link fence and "limbo dance" our way inside.

"Now keep an ear out for dogs," Kyle warns me.

A shudder passes through me. "You really think there might be dogs in here?"

"Don' know, but the place is so big, that's what I'd do if I owned it."

Kyle leads me on a route that stays as far away from the main office as possible. We pass all kinds of junk, just about anything you could imagine—and a lot that you couldn't. There are mountains of wrecked cars, canyons of refrigerators and washing machines, oases of furniture. I see metal shelving, tin roofing, even ripped up lanes from a bowling alley next to a small mountain of bowling pins. Then, we get to the heavy equipment section.

"Wow," I whisper. "Look at these machines. What do

you think they're for?"

From my junior high metal and wood shop classes, I recognize some of them. Things like drills, joiners, saws, and sanders. But there's a lot of equipment that looks totally alien.

"I never seen some 'a this stuff," Kyle says. "But we're gettin' close to the coin press."

We circle around a tangle of pipes and duct work, and Kyle halts.

"Voilà," he says.

"Wow."

Dan Carroll was right. The Bliss press is a monster. It stands at least twelve, fifteen feet high. At first, it looks totally different from Dan's press or the ones we saw at the Denver Mint, but then I start to detect some familiar parts. Mounted high on the right side is a huge flywheel, which stores power for the enormous forces necessary to stamp out coins or ammunition. It also looks like a "knuckle-joint" type of machine, where once the flywheel is engaged, it straightens up the joint to apply pressure to the coin. Unlike the other presses I've seen, however, this one doesn't seem to have as many compartments and moving parts *below* the stamping platform—which doesn't bode well for hidden coins.

"So, where do we start?" I ask.

"Well, I found that one coin in here," Kyle says, pointing to a narrow space between what I guess is a feeding tube and one of the uprights on the machine. "I figure we should start by taking off these little platforms and stuff."

"Sounds good."

"I shoulda brought an extra wrench, but we can take turns."

Kyle sets about unscrewing a series of bolts that fastens the little stages on the machine's main platform.

"Those must be what held the lower dies and the coin collars," I say. "What did Dan call them? The strike block?"

"Think he said 'stake block'," Kyle tells me with a grunt, twisting away at a bolt.

I leave him to his work and slowly walk around the rest of the machine, looking for places that coins or coin blanks might have landed. It's dark enough now that I turn on the flashlight, and I also notice that the lightning is moving closer to us. About twenty seconds after one flash, I hear a faint rumble.

About four miles away, I calculate.

I continue to study the machine. I poke my fingers into some joints and gaps in the moving assembly. This is the area where the obverse, or top, die would have been mounted, and is actually what presses down to strike the coin.

The ram.

Soon, I spot something and walk back to get a screwdriver from Kyle.

"You see anythin'?" he asks, still working on the front cover.

"Maybe."

I return to my spot and slide the screwdriver into the slot and jimmy out a disk, letting it drop into my other hand. My heart is beating fast now, but it is only a nickel-and-copper blank, a little bigger than the one Kyle already found.

Probably used for making a half dollar, I think.

Just then, a few fat drops of rain splatter down onto me.

I keep shining the flashlight all around, but don't find anything else. Something is bothering me about this coin press, and I can't put my finger on it. I've already realized that it's a different design from the others in the Mint, but there's more to it than that.

"Got 'em!" Kyle calls from the other side.

I hurry back around to see Kyle lowering the second of the little platforms to the ground.

"Find anything?"

"Give me the flashlight."

Kyle shines the light into the spaces left behind.

"Look here!"

The flashlight beam illuminates a couple of dozen round objects that have found their way into the cracks next to and underneath the stages.

My hopes rise.

"What denominations are they?" I ask.

"You tell me."

Kyle scoops up a few of the disks and hands them to me, and then starts examining the others himself.

The sky has grown even darker now, but a floodlight about fifty yards away gives me enough light to see by. I squat down next to Kyle and use the pillowcase he brought to wipe away the grease on the coins one by one.

"Watcha got?" Kyle asks.

"Here's a couple of dimes," I tell him. "And three quarters—1960, 1963, and…1961."

"Well, I guess we know when this press was bein' used. I got some Franklin half dollars here."

"Cool. Oh, hey, I've got one, too. 1961. And here are several more coin blanks."

"Anything silver dollar size?"

I look through the coins again. "Well, here's something that looks the right size, but it's made out of copper. Probably for making some kind of medals."

"The Mint makes medals?"

"Yeah. For presidents and war heroes, things like that." I shift over to see what Kyle is looking through. "Did you find any silver dollars?"

I can already guess the answer. If he'd found one, he'd have told me by now.

"Naw," he says. "Here's a quarter that looks like it was hit twice and a dime that the die missed halfway, but no silver dollars."

He hands me the coins he is holding.

"Well, these error coins could be worth some money," I tell him. "Maybe a few hundred bucks."

"Ya think so?"

"Yeah," I say, but disappointment weighs in both of our voices.

Kyle stands up. "What about the rest of the machine?"

"I didn't see much. Come look."

Together, we slowly circle the giant press. Kyle and I both poke into cracks and crevices, and I spot two more coins—dimes—wedged behind a little box attached to the back of the machine. Nothing, however, remotely resembles a silver dollar.

"Well, shoot," Kyle says.

"Yeah."

By now, the rain pounds down on us. Part of me wants to climb up on the machine and keep looking, but I don't see how any of the coins would have ended up way above the ram and stake block.

Suddenly, I hear a dog bark.

"That sounded like it was just across the yard," I hiss.

"Quick. Help me get these stages back in place. Then, let's get out of here."

I don't want to bother putting things back, but realize that Kyle's right to make things look like they're undisturbed. We each take one of the stages and quickly hand-tighten the bolts back in place.

The dog barks again, closer now.

"This way!" Kyle says, scooping up his tools.

I follow him in the opposite direction we came in from. The dog barks again, followed by a second dog.

My adrenaline is pumping like a hydraulic grease gun as Kyle and I both break into a dead run. Even with the pounding rain, I listen for the sounds of running paws and saliva-coated teeth behind me, but before I hear either, we reach another corner of the yard. I don't know how Kyle led us straight here, but I'm not complaining. He quickly snips away the corner of the chain link, and we squeeze through.

The dogs bark again, but the rain seems to have thrown them off our scent.

"Safe," I whisper, as we hurry back toward the Bel Air.

THIRTY-EIGHT

▽

Safe, but not secure.

We reach the Bel Air with drenching rain cascading over us. Drops hit me so hard, I wince as they strike my skin. It reminds me of the hurricane Kyle and I went through on Shipwreck Island two years ago.

I duck into the car to find Annie sitting in the front seat, as if preparing to drive away, so I hop in the back, sloshing water all over the seat. After throwing the tools in the trunk, Kyle flings open the driver's side door.

"Scoot over!" he orders Annie.

"What took you so long?" she exclaims. "I thought you was busted for sure!"

"We weren't that long," Kyle says impatiently, squeezing water out of his hair. "We had to unbolt some of the machine to look into it."

"I heard dogs!"

"Probably just some hungry beagles."

"Well, did ya find somethin'?"

"Struck out."

I don't add anything, but hearing Kyle's words again gives me a strange feeling about the coin press.

It's not that we didn't check out every place on it, I think. *It is more like something is, well, missing.*

Annie smirks. "I knew it. Now let's get outta here."

Kyle starts up the Bel Air. Putting it into gear, he turns to me. "Mike, what you want to do? The bus station?"

I haven't thought that far ahead. Between not finding the Peace dollar and Annie's earlier confession, I feel off-balance, almost dizzy.

I shrug. "I don't know. I was beginning to think we'd really find it."

"Yeah, me too."

"You guys are both dreamers," Annie scoffs.

"Will you shut up?" Kyle tells her, and this time he sounds like he means it.

"Y'all shut up," she shoots back. "This was a stupid idea all along. I don' even know why you listened to Mike in the first place."

Kyle defends me. "It wasn't Mike's fault. If it weren't for him, we wouldn't 'a even got this far."

But I know as well as Annie does that her remark isn't about the silver dollar. It's about our earlier conversation.

"So, Mike," Kyle resumes, trying to ignore her. "What you wanna do?"

Annie flicks on the Bel Air's heater and I feel a wisp of warm air breeze through the back seat.

"What are *you* going to do?" I ask.

"Head north," Kyle tells me. "I been thinkin' Canada's our best bet. We don't need no passports to get in, and I can find me a job, get some work."

"You think they'll let Annie in? She doesn't even have a driver's license."

"I'll talk us through."

"Uh… are you sure?" I have seen Kyle do some amazing things, but I have my doubts that his Southern charm will work on hard-nosed border police used to looking for draft dodgers.

"I'll figure out somethin'. Don't worry about us, Mike. You gotta get back to your family."

I think about my dad, and my mom in California,

and how worried they must be. I sigh deeply. "Okay. The bus station, I guess."

Kyle nods and puts the car in gear.

Rain continues to pound down on the car. So much rain that it runs in shallow rivers across the asphalt. The deluge has almost emptied the streets, and we don't see a single police patrol as we make our way downtown, first on 40th Avenue, then on Blake Street.

Kyle drives slowly while I sit in the back seat with a flashlight, poring over the Denver city map in my lap. I've located the bus terminal on it and tell Kyle which way to turn. As we drive closer, I tell him, "It's on 19th Street. Not too far from Dan's place."

The bus terminal is hard to miss—a squat, ugly building devouring an entire city block. Kyle pulls right up to the front doors in a "No Parking" zone, but in this rain, I doubt anyone's going to come along and give us a ticket.

I glance through the glass doors into the terminal, my gut heavy. Despite not finding a Peace dollar and the confusion Annie's revelation has caused me, I don't want to step out of the car. What Kyle, Annie, and I have gone through in the last seven days, well, it's nothing like my life in Florida, and for sure not in California. It's like I've woken up from some kind of stupor and I for darned sure don't want to go back to sleep.

Kyle looks back at me. "Well?"

My eyes shift from the bus station to him. "Yeah. Well."

"You gotta enough money for a ticket and some food?"

I reach into my pocket and pull out my change.

"I could use another ten."

Annie doesn't even turn her head and Kyle punches her lightly. "Annie, give Mike a twenty."

"Sorry," I tell Kyle. "I know you're going to need it."

Without looking at me, Annie hands Kyle a twenty and he gives it to me. "Wish I could give ya more."

"Here," I tell him. "Take some of these coins we found in the press. You can sell them to a coin shop."

Kyle waves me off. "Naw, I wouldn't know if I was gettin' ripped off. You sell 'em and send me some of the profits."

"How will I find you?"

"I'll send you our address."

I raise an eyebrow at him, and he chuckles. "Really, Mike. This time, I'll make sure you get a good address."

"Okay," I say reluctantly.

Kyle sticks out his hand. "Mike, it's been real. *Again.*"

"Yeah," I say, gripping his hand firmly. "Be careful."

"We will."

Kyle and I keep our hands locked, unwilling to break our grip, but I finally let go.

"Goodbye, Annie."

Annie still doesn't say anything, and Kyle lightly punches her again. "Tell him goodbye, you brat!"

"Bye," she mumbles, still not looking at me.

But as Kyle flings the door open, she suddenly shouts. "Oh my god! Look!"

nnie is pointing into the bus terminal so I look, but don't see anything different from a moment before.

Kyle, though, curses.

"That bastard!"

"Who?" I ask, still sitting in the back seat.

"My uncle!" Annie shouts.

"*What?*"

I study the people I can see through the doors. Way on the far side of the terminal, I spot a tall man wearing a gray hat and a suit, sitting in a chair reading a book.

A Bible! I realize. Without even asking, I know it's their uncle.

"What's he *doing* here, Kyle?" Annie's voice verges on hysterics.

Kyle growls. "I don't know."

"Um, there's something I probably should have told you."

Annie and Kyle both turn around to look at me, question marks on their faces.

I swallow. "Uh, I didn't tell you, but my dad said your uncle was heading out to Denver to look for you."

"*What?*" Annie says. "Why didn't you tell us?"

"I didn't think it mattered," I lamely explain. "I thought the chances of him finding us were pretty much zero, and that it would just make you more worried. Sorry."

Kyle doesn't say anything. Instead, he grips and re-grips the steering wheel, and I can tell by his tense jaw and shoulders that he is calculating. Calculating *what* I'm not exactly sure, but that becomes clear when he suddenly leaps out of the car.

"Where are you going?" I ask.

He growls, "I shoulda taken care of him in Birmingham, but now I'm gonna fix him."

I scramble out of the Bel Air and manage to cut him off at the curb. "Kyle, no!"

"Mike get outta my way! What he did to Annie—"

"Annie!" I shout.

Kyle reaches for my shoulders to move me.

"Annie!" I say, louder. "Tell him!"

Kyle's hands freeze on my shoulders. "Tell me what?"

"Annie?" I repeat.

Finally, I think, Annie has got to tell her brother the truth. But, I'm wrong. Annie doesn't say a word.

Kyle looks toward the car. "Annie, what you got to tell me?"

Still sitting in the front passenger seat, his sister turns away, clearly determined to stay silent. I glance back into the bus terminal to see if their uncle has noticed us outside. Fortunately, the glare of the fluorescent lights off of the glass door seems to be blocking his view of the street.

"Kyle," I say. "Your uncle never beat Annie. He didn't lock her in the closet either."

Kyle's face boils with anger and confusion, and for a moment I think he's going to hit me. "'Course he did. Mike, what're you sayin'?"

"No. He didn't."

"You callin' my sister a liar?"

"Kyle, she told me herself!"

"She…"

And slowly, the fire goes out of Kyle. His shoulders slump and he looks to his sister. "Annie, that true?"

Again, Annie says nothing, but this time, she doesn't have to. Kyle spins away from me and slams his hand down hard on the hood of the Bel Air. Then, he reaches up and puts his hand over his face.

Finally, Annie rolls down her window and says, "We gotta get outta here."

Whatever else he's feeling and thinking, Kyle agrees. He strides back around to the driver's side and gets in. Without even thinking about it, I go to the opposite door and open it. Annie hops into the back seat and I take her place in front.

As the car roars away from the curb, none of us say anything. Then, Kyle explodes. "Annie! How could you make up a story like that?"

"Most of it was true!"

"*Most of it?* That's like sayin' most of it is okay—and it ain't! It ain't even close! Man, what are we gonna do now?"

My own mind has been racing, trying to answer that very same question. "Kyle pull over somewhere," I tell him.

"What?"

"Pull over. Just do it."

He turns right, down a side street, and stops the Bel Air. He turns to me, his face twisted with emotion. "Mike, what? You wanna go back to the bus station?"

And to his surprise, I answer. "Yeah. I do."

"Fine," he says and shifts the Bel Air back into first.

"No, wait. Listen to me," I say. "I've got an idea, but first I have to ask you a question."

"What?"

"Are you going to take Annie back to Alabama?"

"No!" Annie pleads from the back seat.

"Because if you are," I continue. "I think you and your uncle can talk things out—but only if you tell him about the story Annie made up."

"Kyle, no! I can't go back there! Please don't make me!"

Even though Annie has led us all on, I believe the desperation in her voice. Kyle must, too.

"No," he says. "It's too late for that now."

"That's what I figured," I say. "So, I've got a plan."

"What plan?"

I take a deep breath and tell them both what I have in mind. My plan has a few holes in it, and I'm not at all sure how it will play out, but I manage to convince Kyle and Annie that it's worth a try.

After I finish explaining, they drive me back to the bus terminal.

Kyle looks at me. "Mike, you sure about this?"

I shrug. "Who knows? It might work."

Kyle nods. "Okay. Good luck."

"If I don't end up in jail, I'll see you in a few," I tell them, opening the passenger door and stepping out. While the Bel Air drives away, I walk into the bus station.

FORTY

At first I don't see Kyle's and Annie's uncle, but then I notice that he's moved to another chair and is drinking a cup of coffee as he studies people coming in and out of the station. He gives me a quick once over, but there's no reason he should recognize me, and his gaze moves on.

I follow the plan that I hurriedly outlined to Kyle, and proceed to the ticket window, where I ask for a one-way ticket back to Pensacola. The fare runs most of what I have in my pocket, but I can't do anything about that. After getting my ticket and change, I turn and walk over to Kyle's and Annie's uncle, who has gone back to reading the Bible. I clear my throat, and he looks up.

"Excuse me, you're Mr. Taylor, Annie's uncle, aren't you?"

A startled look crosses his face and he snaps the Bible shut.

"How did you know that?"

"I'm Mike."

I wondered if I'd have to explain, but he practically leaps from his seat.

"Where's Annie?" he demands.

The man is even taller than I'd thought—six-three, six-four, at least—and he uses it to his advantage. He steps close to me and looks down through spectacles that magnify his angry, red eyes. I instantly dislike the man, and as much as I fight it, feel more than a little intimidated.

"They're not here," I croak.

"Son," his harsh voice rumbles, "d'you have any conception of how much trouble y'all are in?"

With this angry, threatening man towering over me, the script I'd written for this conversation flies from my head, and I stand there without answering.

"Do you know how worried your daddy is?"

Guilt starts to wash up through me, but then something else replaces it. Suddenly, I realize something about Mr. Taylor that I should have guessed earlier.

This man is a bully.

I don't know why that surprises me. After all, I've seen my fair share of bullies at school, and even in my own home. My stepfather's one of the biggest I ever met. And even though I don't approve of the lies Annie told, I suddenly understand them. In a flash, I also understand how I need to handle her uncle. What I say next surprises even myself.

"My dad and me are none of your business."

"You address me by 'sir', son."

And now, any sympathy I have for the guy totally evaporates.

"I'm not your son, and I'll call you whatever I want."

The man steps even closer. "Look here, boy, one call to the police and your ass is cooked. If you want to stay out of the slammer, you tell me where Annie and that no-good brother of hers are, and you tell me *now!*"

A year ago, a month ago, maybe even yesterday, I would have done what he said—or at least run away in fear. But a switch has been thrown inside me. Even though I'm trembling, I look him straight in the eye. "You call whoever you want. You tell them your side of the story, and I'll tell them mine, and we'll see who they believe. But if you do that, I *guarantee* you will never see Annie again."

For the first time, the man's eyes flicker with doubt. His teeth grind, and he asks. "You know where they are?"

"Maybe."

"Don't play games with me, boy," he says, but his threats no longer bother me. For the first time in my life, I've got a bully right where I want him.

"I *don't* play games, not like you do."

"I want to see them."

This is exactly what I want to hear, but I don't give myself away.

"Why?" I ask. "So you can take Annie back and keep being mean to her? So you can keep telling her she's going to hell if she doesn't do exactly what *you* say? So you can keep her locked up in the house?"

Uncle Taylor suddenly notices that people are looking at us. His face turns crimson and he says, "N-no. We are her legal guardians. She belongs with us!"

"She's not *ever* going back with you," I tell him. "But if I can find them, maybe I can get them to meet you."

"Will you do it?" he asks, his voice suddenly syrupy.

That's typical of a bully, too, I think. *If they can't intimidate you, they try to butter you up.*

"I don't know."

"Please. It's important. My wife and I are worried sick over that little gal."

Oh, please. You're worried about your reputation, you phony.

"Do you promise to call off the police?" I ask.

"Well, son," he says, spreading his hands helplessly. "There's only so much I can do."

"Not if you tell them you found her and that she's safe with you."

"I—" The man is doing his own quick calculations, but I can read what he's thinking.

I tell him, "If you think the police will find them first, you're wrong. Annie and Kyle are somewhere no one will find them, so you either strike a deal with me or you're out of luck." For added emphasis, I wave my Greyhound ticket at him. "My bus for Florida leaves in an hour. I am just as happy to get on it, and you'll never see any of us again."

A protracted silence stretches between us. Finally the man's shoulders sag and he says, "You win."

I take a breath, but try not to betray my relief.

"Okay. Come to the terminal at about this same time tomorrow night. Ten p.m. I'll try to convince Annie and Kyle to meet you. But if we see any police or anything else, you'll never see them again."

"No funny stuff. I promise," he says.

As I turn away from him, I think, *Yeah, right.*

FORTY-ONE

On my way out of the Greyhound station, I spot a stand displaying city bus schedules, and grab a couple. By the time I'm back on the street, it's almost eleven p.m. I walk a block and then stop to scan the area, making sure no one is following me.

Just like a detective movie, I think with a smile.

The streets are clear, so I hurry on to where I told Kyle to pull over earlier. I am relieved to see the Bel Air sitting there waiting.

When she sees me, Annie crawls over into the back.

"How'd he look?" Annie asks as I open the front passenger door. "Was he mad?"

"*Mad* isn't the word. I see why you don't like him."

Before I can elaborate, Kyle cuts in. "What'd he say?"

"I think he bought it," I tell them both. "The meeting's on for ten p.m. tomorrow."

Kyle leans back in his seat. "Good. Thanks, Mike."

I shrug. "Just because he agreed to it, doesn't mean that's what he's going to do."

"Yeah, but it buys us time to get outta here."

Which was the whole point. My plan was to make Mr. Taylor think that we—or at least Kyle and Annie—were going to stay in the city at least another twenty-four hours. That would give Kyle and Annie a day's worth of head start to Canada or wherever they decide to go. But now, I'm having second—and maybe third or fourth—thoughts about that idea.

"So, Mike, what you gonna do?" Kyle asks.

"Uh, well I was just going to give it an hour and then catch my bus to Florida."

"But what?"

I look over at Kyle. "Huh?"

"I can tell you're thinkin' something', Big Mike. What is it?"

"Well..." I glance back at Annie. "It's about you two getting into Canada. The more I think about it, the more I think they're going to stop you. Maybe worse."

"Whaddya mean?" Annie asks, leaning forward from the back seat.

"Annie, you're only thirteen. They're not going to let Kyle—your *brother*—take you into another country."

"But I can pass for eighteen," she says. "You said so yourself."

"It don't matter," Kyle joins in. "Mike's right. I been thinkin' on it, too. Unless we got papers, it ain't gonna work. I got my papers declaring I'm my own guardian, but you—"

"They're not going to let you across," I finish for him.

"Well, then we'll go to California," Annie says brightly. "I like that better 'n Canada anyway."

I shake my head. "Look, once you miss that meeting with your uncle tomorrow night, it's going to be all-out war. He's going to pull every string he can think of to find you."

"So, you gotta new plan?" Kyle asks me.

I pause. "Yeah, maybe. It's risky, though. It means you're going to have to spend another night here in Denver. You might not even get out of town much earlier than when you're supposed to meet your uncle tomorrow."

Kyle thoughtfully scratches his day-old beard. Finally, he says, "Well, I don't see what we got to lose. You gonna stay with us?"

"Yeah. I have to. Besides, there's one more thing I want to do."

Kyle drives back to the abandoned sheet-metal factory where we spent the afternoon. None of us looks forward to sleeping in the Bel Air again, especially in clothes that are starting to stink after being worn for three days straight. The only thing that makes it easier is knowing that one way or another, this is all going to be over soon. Very soon.

We again let Kyle stretch out on the front seat while Annie and I divide up the back. After all that's been said in the last twenty-four hours, the thought of cuddling together doesn't even cross my mind, and I'm sure it doesn't cross Annie's, either. Still, as I listen to the rhythmic ticking of the Bel Air engine cooling down, I feel like some kind of truce has been called between us. After meeting Annie's uncle myself, I still don't think she was right to lie about him, but I do understand more why she felt like she had to. Even though he never physically abused Annie, I can't imagine living with the guy, and if I can't, it's got to be twice as tough for Annie.

Thinking about him again also makes me think about my own stepfather. He's nowhere near as bad as Annie's uncle.

But they're cut from the same cloth, I think. *They're both bullies who try to push people around any way they can.*

And replaying my interaction with Uncle Taylor, I realize that even though I did that for Kyle and Annie, it's done something for me, too. It's made me realize that I don't have to take crap from a bully, even a grown-up.

I finally fall asleep to the rumble of freight trains on the Union Pacific track a few blocks away. I am so exhausted, I sleep right through sunrise a few hours later. When Kyle's hand does jostle me awake, I am surprised to see the Bel Air sitting in the full light of morning.

"What time is it?" I mumble, sitting up. I look over to find Annie's seat empty.

"Almost eight," Kyle says.

"Where's Annie?"

"Off takin' care of business, but we're hungry. Let's go pick up some food."

"You go ahead," I say, quickly waking up. "But drop me at the scrap yard first."

Kyle looks at me impatiently. "Mike, we checked all over that coin press. Ain't nothin' there."

"I know," I tell him. "I'm just going to take a minute. After you get some food, come back here and wait for me. If I don't show up by five o'clock at the latest, I won't be coming. You get out of Denver as fast as you can."

"You're sure about this?"

"Who knows? But I'll try to get back here a lot earlier."

That seems to satisfy Kyle.

"Okay," he tells me. "Take a screwdriver with you."

FORTY-TWO

I've never entered the scrap yard through the front door, and I almost blow it. As I walk into the low, cheaply-made building that serves as the entrance, I am stopped by a crusty old geezer wearing a blue button-down work shirt and an International Harvester cap.

"What do you need?" he barks at me, and I realize I should have prepared an answer ahead of time.

Thinking fast, I come up with about the stupidest response possible. "Oh, uh, someone told me you had some, uh, bowling pins somewhere."

"I got 'em. What do you want 'em for?"

"I'm, uh…learning to juggle."

His scowl bores into me, and I'm thinking, *He's going to kick me out of here—or call the police! Maybe he knows that Kyle and I broke into his place last night!*

My thoughts are about to really gallop away from me, when he pulls out a stick of gum and begins to unwrap it.

"You know," he tells me, eyes narrowing. "Those pins are a darn sight heavier than you'd expect. You think you can really juggle with them? A scrawny kid like you?"

The tone of his voice clearly indicates he'd bet ten-to-one odds against it, but it at least gives me an opening.

I puff out my chest and say, "Sure I can—but only if they're the right kind."

He snorts and to my surprise, cracks a smile. "Well have at it then. There's a whole pile of pins straight back about a hundred yards. And you're in luck. I got 'em on special today—ten bucks for as many as you can carry."

He laughs as his own cleverness and I hurry on into the yard.

I actually do find the bowling pins, and can't resist stopping to pick one up. Hefting it in my hand, I'm guessing it weighs three or four pounds, and I'm almost tempted to buy a few—just to show the geezer that I'm stronger than he thinks. But I've got bigger fish to fry today—or at least bigger lanes to bowl.

Tossing the pin back in the pile, I get my bearings and quickly locate the giant, industrial-gray coin press. In the broad daylight, the machine is even more impressive than it was last night. Up on top of the press are stenciled the words "BLISS 23B" in large white letters, and I stop to reflect on the fact that this machine actually used to make real ammunition for our troops in World War II. I reach my hand out to touch the steel, still cold from last night. As I trace my fingers all around the machine, visions of marines landing on remote Pacific islands, ducking under machine gun fire, fill my head.

But that doesn't mean I've forgotten why I came.

After a once-around the coin press, I confirm that there are no more places a coin—and a silver dollar specifically—could have slipped down into a nook or cranny. But last night, walking from the bus station to the Bel Air, it had suddenly occurred to me why something seemed wrong about this machine when Kyle and I searched it before. Something was missing.

The control panels.

Dan Carroll's coin press had at least two separate control panels that went along with his coin press. One, he showed us, was an electrical junction box. The other was some kind of signal box that indicated when everything was working properly.

Last night, I didn't notice anything like that on the Bliss press. Today, in broad daylight, however, I can see a spot on the machine's upper right-side where the paint is a darker shade of gray than the rest of the press.

Like something's been removed, I think.

I turn away from the machine and start searching all around it. At first I am not sure where to start. This is a scrap yard, after all, and piles of junk sit everywhere. But in a heap of assorted metal frames and cases, I notice a metal box painted the same color as the Bliss press.

My heart ticks faster. I am not sure what I'm expecting to find, but several thoughts have occurred to me. One is that if an employee really wanted to swipe a Peace dollar or other coin, it might be kind of stupid to just try to walk out with it—especially after, as Dan said, they tightened up security procedures.

A better way might be to hide the coin on or near the presses and then wait for an opportunity to come back and get it later.

I know it's still a long shot that something like that happened, but as I reach for the metal box, my fingers tremble with the possibility.

The box stretches maybe two feet tall, a foot and a half wide, and six inches deep. A metal tube pokes up out of the top, with several bundles of green, yellow, and black wires hanging out the end, and the whole front face of the box acts like a door. I pick up the entire box and tilt it against a couple of cinder blocks. I glance around, but no one is in sight, so I quickly open the door to see several buttons and dials, each with their own little housings screwed to the back of the box.

The perfect place to hide a coin.

I reach into the box and feel all around. Then, I look back inside and do another search of the box. Nothing.

"Crap," I mutter. But then I notice a larger object partially obscured by another pile of scrap metal. Leaving the electronics panel, I hurry over to the other thing. I'm not sure what I'm looking at. It's like a large metal box with some kind of machinery on top of it. The object looks heavy—at least a couple of hundred pounds—and I'm guessing it's a compressor of some kind. By the paint color, it definitely looks like it belongs with the Bliss press.

I search all of the exposed parts of the equipment, but don't find anything. There's also a panel opening into the base, however, sealed closed by screws.

Thank you, Kyle, I think, pulling the screwdriver from my back pocket. Again making sure no one is watching, I race to remove the screws. Now, my heart thunders. I can't tell if it's because I'm afraid someone will catch me or because I realize that this may be an even better hiding place than the electronics panel.

When I remove the last screw, I pry open the door. An old yellowed piece of paper with some kind of instructions is taped to the inside, but I don't have time to read them. Instead, I peer into the little space. One thing I didn't bring with me is a flashlight, but I see a jumble of tubes and pipes inside. I don't spot any coins or packages so I reach in and run my fingers all along the pipes. Grease and grime quickly coat my fingertips, but I keep probing and exploring the guts of the equipment, expecting to touch silver any second.

It doesn't happen.

"Shoot!" I exclaim, peering into the compressor-thing

one last time. Disappointed, I stand up and try to shake it off, but it's not as easy as I expected.

I really thought I'd find it this time.

I try to laugh at my own optimism, but the laugh doesn't make it past my throat.

I pick up the screwdriver and start back toward the entrance. As I pass through the shadow of the giant Bliss press, however, I have one last pie-in-the-sky idea. I hurry back to the electronics box I already searched and open it again. I closely study the dials and buttons, and for the first time, I notice that their little housings sit up off of the back of the box by a fraction of an inch. Only two screws hold each housing in place.

As I start unscrewing the first one, I'm not expecting to find anything.

This is just so I never have to think about it again, I tell myself.

And sure enough, the first housing yields no surprises. Nothing is hidden behind it.

I move on to the second. I remove the top screw, then the bottom. Years of grease and grime seem to have sealed the button housing to the back of the electronics box, so I reach in and give it a little tug. And as it breaks free, I hear something slide down to the bottom of the box and hit it with a soft, metallic *plunk*.

FORTY-THREE

There, in the bottom of the metal box lies a folded up square of paper, about two inches on a side. I blink twice to make sure I'm really seeing it. With my imagination, it's not too far-fetched to think I'm making it up. But the thing is there. No question about it.

I wipe my fingers on my pants, and reach for the small paper packet. As trains of neurons fire throughout my body, I hold the packet in one hand and carefully peel back the folds of paper with the other. When I peel back the last fold, I sharply suck in my breath.

Resting in my left palm is the glittering image of a perched eagle with the words "ONE DOLLAR" stamped on either side of its tail. The eagle's posture is bold, even aggressive, and its beak and head glint in the glare of the morning Mile-High sun. Just as important, I see a small letter "D" stamped into the disk right at the tip of the eagle's tail.

But even though I know that I am holding a silver dollar—a silver dollar minted in Denver—I still don't know if I'm holding *the* silver dollar. And honestly, I'm not sure I can stand the excitement of finding out.

Taking another deep breath, however, I slowly turn the silver dollar over.

"Yes!"

There she is—the determined, crowned head of Liberty herself, staring determinedly to the West. Her hair is tousled as if blowing in the breezes of victory and conquest, adversity and invention, the words "IN GOD WE

TRUST" engraved alongside her neck. But it's what I see stamped along the bottom rim of the coin that makes all the difference. The difference between just another cartwheel and a piece of history.

The date 1964.

And believe me, that date means *everything*.

I wrap the coin back up and stick it into my pocket. Then, I check the other buttons and dials to see if coins are hidden behind them, too. As much as I wish otherwise, I find nothing. I close the panel door, and without wasting any more time, quickly stand and rush back to the scrap yard entrance.

"Find anything?" the crusty proprietor asks me.

"You were right," I tell him. "Those bowling pins are too heavy."

He smirks. "Told you!"

Back out in front, I sprint along the road toward the nearest major thoroughfare about a third of a mile away. It feels good to run again. I stretch out my legs and accelerate, pushing my stiff, reluctant body into a familiar rhythm. I could easily cover the distance back to the Bel Air in ten, fifteen minutes tops.

But I'm not going to the Bel Air. Instead of returning to Kyle and Annie, I find the nearest bus stop and catch the next bus that comes, heading downtown.

It takes me longer than I hope to get everything done, but I do finish it all. Once Dan Carroll and I complete our business, he lets me borrow his car—a souped up '69 Camaro. I stop by a department store and a travel agent, and then head back to the abandoned factory to pick up Annie and Kyle. We leave the Bel Air at the factory and then head for the terminal.

Despite the rush hour traffic, we arrive early. I park next to the curb and turn off the Camaro's engine.

"Nice wheels," Kyle repeats.

"Not as nice as the Bel Air, but it'll do."

Kyle chuckles. "So tell me again why you thought to go back to the scrap yard?"

"Well," I explain. "After we struck out looking for coins hidden in the machine, I thought about if I'd been a Mint employee. How much I would have loved to have a 1964-D Peace dollar for myself—not that I ever would have stolen one, mind you."

Kyle grins. "'Course not."

"So anyway," I continue. "I realized that after Dan's co-worker got hit by the bus and they found the stolen cartwheel in his pocket, the only way to make off with a Peace dollar would be to stash the coin somewhere inside the Mint and maybe come back for it later."

"You mean 'cause security got tighter then, and they woulda caught anyone tryin' to just carry it out."

"That's right. But if they hid the coin, then they could wait until security eased up again, and then sneak it out later. The question was, where to stash the coin?"

"The Mint working floor looked pretty clean," Kyle says.

"That's right, but those presses are complicated, with lots of hiding places."

"And that's when you realized not all of the press was there last night?"

I nod. "At least not where we could see it. Today, though, in full sunlight, I spotted that electronics panel and my heart about jumped out of my chest."

"Aw, c'mon," Annie says. "You didn't really think you'd find a coin in there, did ya?"

"No," I admit. "But I hoped I would."

"And you got lucky."

Kyle throws his head back and laughs out loud. "Luck don't begin to describe it, do it Mike?"

I also laugh. "Not even close."

"So, anyway, here's the cash." I hand Kyle an envelope stuffed with hundred dollar bills. "I took out about a thousand. I hope you don't mind."

"I still think you should keep half of it," Kyle tells me.

I shake my head. "You guys need it more. A lot more."

Next, I hand each of them their tickets, and Annie her new passport.

She opens the document. "Leslie Carroll?"

"Dan's daughter," I explain. "It was his idea. After I sold him the coin, he gave me the passport. Said he didn't really think his daughter was ever coming back, and that you looked enough like her that you could get away with it."

"This picture don't look nothin' like me," Annie objects.

Kyle takes it from her. "Yeah, it does, Sis. Especially when you was younger."

"I agree," I tell her. "I don't think you'll have any trouble passing as his daughter. Just memorize all the details on the passport. Address. Parents' names. All of it. The ticket's in her name—your new name—so don't screw up."

Kyle turns and gives her a mock glare. "She won't."

We sit there silently for a moment and a jet roars over our heads.

"Our uncle is going to flip when we don't show up,"

Annie says.

"It's not my fault," I say. "I said meet back at the terminal. I didn't tell him we were coming to the airline terminal instead of the bus station."

Kyle snorts appreciatively.

"You'll be in Calgary in about three hours," I tell them. "With luck, you'll be sleeping between clean sheets tonight."

"Thanks for buyin' us the suitcases and clothes," Kyle says.

"I just thought you'd attract less suspicion. And since you've now got separate names, no one ought to be expecting you."

Kyle nods. "Good. But Mike, I'm sorry you didn't get to keep that Peace dollar. I know how much you wanted it."

I shrug. "It's illegal to own anyway."

"Dan know that?"

I laugh. "He doesn't care! He just wanted it."

"How'd you know he'd have the money?"

"I just figured he would. He didn't look like he was hurting, and every serious coin guy I've ever met seems to have cash around for emergencies. Besides, he told me straight out he could flip the Peace dollar to another collector for four, five times as much."

Kyle smiles appreciatively. "Well, glad to know it's got a good home."

We sit silently for another moment, then Kyle opens the door and gets out. "C'mon Annie. Time to go."

I walk back to the trunk and open it. I reach in and hand Kyle and Annie their new suitcases.

"Kyle," I say, sticking out my hand.

He grabs it. "Mike. Catch ya across the border."

"Yeah. Just tell me when you're all set up."

Then, I turn to his sister. "Annie?"

Her chin is down, but she lifts her eyes in my direction. They hold a far away look, but no resentment. She's probably already thinking about Canada, worrying what she's going to do there. I don't blame her. I'd be thinking the same thing.

"Take care of yourself," I tell her. "And take care of Kyle, okay?"

With that, she comes back, at least part way.

"You, too," she says. "I mean, I will."

She gives me a little smile, and with that, they both turn and walk into Stapleton Airport.

FORTY-FOUR

Later That Night

I'm driving through western Nebraska. It's not the shortest way back to Florida, but Kyle thought it'd be safer, with fewer people around, and fewer cops looking for me and the Bel Air. So far, I think he's right. I'm cruising a long stretch of highway that probably won't curve until I pass through the entire state into Missouri, and the only other traffic I see are trucks doing the long haul, minding their own business.

The sun went down about two hours ago, and I probably ought to pull over and sleep. I am too keyed up for that. Instead, I sip on a cold cup of coffee and fiddle with the radio dial, looking for a good rock station. It's my bad luck that country-western clutters the airwaves around here.

That's okay. I finally let the dial rest on a song about how a man loves his pickup truck more than his girlfriend and I ponder the events of the last few days. Every once in a while I laugh out loud at certain thoughts. At other times, my eyes grow damp. I worry about Kyle and Annie, and wonder if they made it into Canada safely. I think about the Peace dollar, and ask myself if their Uncle Taylor has figured out what happened by now.

I also think about my parents, both my mom and my dad. After dropping off Kyle and Annie, I'd called them both. My ears still burn from some of the things they said, and I've got more than a little guilt to deal with. What I heard mostly, though, was worry—not disapproval—in their voices. If positions were reversed, I'm not sure I would have restrained myself as much as they did.

I need to try harder with them, I tell myself. Like all parents, they are plenty screwed up, but I realize that unlike some parents, they do their best.

Which is about all anybody can do.

More than my parents, or the trouble I'm in, however, I think about the adventure of the past few days. The towns we passed through, and the people we met. Kyle's friendship, common sense, and courage under pressure. Annie's stubbornness and impatience—and, of course, her chapped lips and the way we held each other for warmth under a thin blanket.

And those are some pretty wonderful thoughts to mull over. Even though I've got a ton of uncertainty and repercussion staring at me, for right now, right this moment, my spirits are light. There's not a place I'd rather be than here, watching the broken white stripes flicker by on the road, feeling the quiet comfort of cornfields and cattle yards in the darkness on either side of me.

A road sign flashes by.

Omaha 323 miles. Kansas City 450.

"Enough of this country music garbage," I say, and reach under the front seat. I pull out one of Kyle's eight-track tapes and flick on the dome light. The tape I'm holding is the one by The Outlaws, the group Annie mentioned that I'd never heard of before.

"Why not?" I mutter and pop it into the player.

I like how it begins. A slow electric guitar playing a haunting riff. Then it repeats, speeding up, building up tension. Other guitars and drums join in, and within moments, a sweet, searing rock-and-roll jam fills my ears, spilling out onto the dark highway racing by.

"That's more like it!" I exclaim, slapping the front dash.

As the music grows more and more frenzied, my grin spreads wider and wider. Letting go of my fear, I shift into fourth gear, press down on the accelerator, and feel the Bel Air respond with a roar, hungry to chew up asphalt.

I grip the steering wheel more tightly, and watch the RPM needle climb above 5500.

"Okay, baby," I shout into the night. "Show me what you can do."

The End

Author's Notes

Having grown up during the Vietnam War and Watergate, I never would have imagined that the 1960s and '70s would be considered "history". Researching *Cartwheel*, however, showed me just how much the world has changed in the last fifty years—and how much information has either been lost, or become difficult to obtain. As in *Double Eagle*, though, this book launched me on a research adventure that proved both enjoyable and fascinating.

When I finished *Double Eagle*, I did not intend to write a sequel. Two events changed my mind. One was that I had the pleasure of visiting Daniel Carr, owner of the Moonlight Mint. A superb artist and designer, Daniel bought a surplus coin press from the United States Mint at Denver several years ago. He got it operational again and has been using it to produce his own beautiful coins (see www.moonlightmint.com). While he was restoring the coin press, however, he discovered hundreds of coin blanks and coins that had fallen into various crevices and cracks, or just been forgotten in the feeder tubes. These were all left over from U.S. Mint operations and, evidently, no one had bothered checking the machine before it was sold.

The other thing Daniel did is mint his own (non-legal tender) 1964-D Peace dollars. Before he did this, I had never heard the story of the real 1964 dollars, but Daniel's fantasy issue got me looking into it. I was astonished to learn that, in 1965, the U.S. Mint at Denver had actually produced more than a *quarter million* silver dollars (some say closer to 400,000) and then, for years, tried to keep it a secret from the public.

Learning of this, I thought, "Ah-ha! There's a story here." At first, I planned to work this new idea into my Slate Stephens Mysteries series. I quickly realized, though, that it would make the perfect sequel to *Double Eagle*.

I decided to set *Cartwheel* in 1975, two years after Mike's and Kyle's previous adventure ended. Little did I know just how many details I would have to unearth to make the story come alive. These included, but weren't limited to: how to soup up a '57 Bel Air; where to eat in Birmingham, Alabama in 1975; what machines were used to mint the 1964 Peace dollars; where the bus station was located in Denver; and a host of other facts. Fortunately, I enlisted a legion of experts to help me out.

To learn about cars and drag-racing in Alabama, I relied on my childhood best friend Eric Dawson, his fellow motorhead Ronald Coby, my own mechanical team at Master Technology Inc. in Missoula, and two wonderful educators in Oneonta, Alabama, Donna Martin and her husband Dennis, whose stories about Blackwell Bottoms feature prominently in the book.

To learn about the Bliss presses used to mint the silver dollars, as well as the actual operation itself, I first read Roger W. Burdette's excellent book *A Guide Book of Peace Dollars*. Dan Savage and Steve Phillips at BCN Technical Services Inc. in Hastings, Michigan were also kind enough to provide me with hard-to-obtain technical specifications for the Bliss presses. I knew, though, that I needed to get a better first-hand feel for what the whole Peace dollar project must have been like, so I booked a flight to Denver.

At the U.S. Mint, I had the generous cooperation of Ellen Casey, Guillermo Hernandez, and Tom Fesing, who led me on a private tour and discussion of Mint operations back in the 1960s and '70s. I was even more fortunate to locate and speak with former Mint employee Michael P. Lanz. Mike worked as a die setter during the actual production of the Peace dollars and provided myriad priceless details about the operation and the Mint in general.

My trip to Denver, of course, also allowed me to visit— and figure out—other locations that appear in the book. Trips to Alabama and Missouri helped fill in additional details.

Still, I couldn't have completed this project without the help of many other people including:

✎ Mitchie and Les Neel, Oneonta, Alabama

✎ Michael Jacquier, Erin Rush, and Dave Fellows at Master-tech, Missoula, Montana

✎ Birmingham History Center (see Bhamwiki.com), Alabama

✎ Russell Wells, Birmingham Rewound

✎ Richard Garza, Sheriff, Hamilton County, Kansas

✎ Leanne Larson, Warrensburg Chamber of Commerce, Missouri

✎ Melody Melloy, Poplar Bluff Chamber of Commerce, Missouri

✎ Paulette Parpart, Missoula Public Library

✎ Jason Huntsinger, Army Navy Economy Store, Missoula, Montana

✎ Stan Berry, Editor, *Daily American Republic*, Poplar Bluff, Missouri

✎ Nancy at Payless Car Rental, Denver International Airport, Colorado

✎ Lori Devanaussi at the Colorado Historical Society, Denver, Colorado

✎ Brian and Erin at the Denver Public Library, Colorado

✎ Kerry Harrington, Santa Barbara, California

✎ Richard Moser, Santa Barbara, California

✎ Gene Nicolelli, Director, Greyhound Bus Museum, Hibbing, Minnesota

✎ Donny Ray and Amy Wilson, Oneonta Chamber of Commerce, Alabama

✎ Jody Georgeson, Director, The Telecommunications History Group, Inc., Denver, Colorado

✎ Sherry Steinbacher, NHRA Motorsports Museum, Pomona, California

✎ Rhody Downey (see http:www.roadrunnercoyote.com),

whose sharp editorial eye helped cut the fat out of the story and reconcile inconsistencies

✎ Kathy Herlihy-Paoli for once again turning my book into a work of art

✎ ✎ ✎ My wife Amy and children, Braden and Tessa

As much research as I did, it's a safe bet that I still got a few things wrong. In our fast-paced world, it is remarkable just how quickly things are lost and replaced. I invite anyone who was there to please write to me with any further recollections or corrections.

I also need to acknowledge that I changed several details for the sake of drama or practical expedience. I "enlarged" Blount County to include the Interstate-65 onramp where Kyle gets pulled over by the sheriff's deputy. Street racers probably wouldn't have "roasted the meat" to warm up their tires unless they had "slick" tires or "cheater slicks". The Denver bus station described in the book did not open until 1976, a year after this story takes place. (The older bus station, at 1730 Glenarm, is now a dismal-looking parking garage and would not have worked well for the story.) McDonald's drive-thrus were just being built in 1975, so Denver's probably wouldn't have had one yet.

Another embellishment is that, according to Michael P. Lanz, security at the Mint was a bit more relaxed than I describe it in 1965. "No one paid attention to the press operators," he told me in a phone interview. This, of course, only adds to the tantalizing thought that one or more of these historical, fascinating 1964 Peace dollars may have survived.

Despite the book's shortcomings, I hope that I've succeeded in giving readers a genuine feel for what the world was like a scant four decades ago. Even more, I hope I've created a story that you will enjoy, think about, and return to again and again.

—*Sneed B. Collard III*

ABOUT THE AUTHOR

Sneed B. Collard III is the author of more than sixty books for young readers including the acclaimed novels *Dog Sense, Double Eagle, The Governor's Dog is Missing,* and *Hangman's Gold.* In addition to his fiction, Sneed has written dozens of outstanding nonfiction children's books including *Animal Dads, Pocket Babies and Other Amazing Marsupials, Shep—Our Most Loyal Dog,* and *The World Famous Miles City Bucking Horse Sale,* also available from Bucking Horse Books. In 2006, Sneed was awarded the prestigious Washington Post-Children's Book Guild Nonfiction Award for his body of work.

When he is not writing, Sneed can often be found speaking to students, teachers, and librarians across the country. To learn more about him or to set up a school or conference visit, go to his website, www.sneedbcollardiii. com or the website of Bucking Horse Books, www.buckinghorsebooks.com.